Sleeping Dogs Lie

Sleeping Dogs Lie

Sharon Henegar

Saturday Books

This book is a work of fiction. Names, characters, places and incidents are the product of the author's imagination or are used fictitiously. Any resemblance to actual events, locales or persons, living or dead, is coincidental.

Published by Saturday Books
PO Box 15952
Santa Ana, CA 92735

ISBN 978-0-9840648-4-7
Library of Congress Control Number: 2010902070
Henegar, Sharon L.
Sleeping dogs lie / Sharon L. Henegar
McGuire, Louisa (Fictitious Character)—Fiction
Antique Dealers—Fiction
Hypnotists—Fiction
Humorous Fiction
Mystery Fiction

Cover design by Lauren Dingus

Sleeping Dogs Lie

1

Sometimes life turns on the smallest decision. On a Monday evening in October it came down to the fact that I chose to wear my black velveteen sneakers embroidered with silver moons and stars, and a storm blew in and poured buckets of rain.

Bob steered his car into the grocery store parking lot and found a slot half-way down the row. "Do you want to come in with me?" he asked. "I'll only be a minute. I need to get some dog food for Jack."

I opened the door and saw a good-sized puddle. I thought of my shoes. "I'll wait." The door made a solid thunk as I pulled it back.

His quick smile flashed. "I'll leave my keys in case you want to listen to the radio." He got out and locked the door behind him. The supermarket's neon signs colored the raindrops that sparkled on his hair as he hurried inside.

I turned on the radio. The familiar clipped tones of the public radio station's news commentator filled the air. I poked the buttons—all rock music or jazz. The only one tuned the same on both our cars was that first public station, and I wondered about the viability of a relationship based on mutual NPR membership. I began to search for classical music, got sidetracked by a country number I'd always liked, paused for the last bars of a Celtic fiddle tune, and finally found a station playing Copland.

The windows of the little Civic had steamed over as soon as the defroster went off. I wiped off the window with my sleeve, and sat back in my seat to listen, looking idly toward the door of the supermarket.

Bob came out, closely followed by a curvy blonde woman in a red business suit and red four-inch heels. She walked with a lithe strut that had no trouble keeping pace with his long-legged steps. I looked down at myself—my black slacks and sweater were comfortable and looked nice, but in a bright red suit I knew I'd feel as wide as a barn door. And those shoes would tip me right onto my nose before I took a single step. I peered down fondly at my fancy sneakers and thought, even if I don't want to get them wet, at least I can walk without injury.

I looked back out at Bob. He was empty handed. No dog food. Had he lost his wallet? He had it earlier when he paid for our dinners. He walked with the woman to a gray Mercedes sedan, an older, classic looking thing, parked in the short row in front of the store. She handed him some keys and said something, and he leaned down to unlock the passenger door.

"What is he doing?" I wondered out loud. The woman stood very close to him. Her right hand jammed into her jacket pocket caused her arm to bend awkwardly. She moved forward to speak directly into his ear. Bob pulled open the door, folding his long legs to get in. He slid over behind the wheel as she seated herself on the passenger side. Exhaust plumed into the night as the engine started.

"Hey!" I yelled, though they couldn't possibly have heard me. I wiped off steam again and squinted at the other car. Maybe it was someone who just looked like Bob—another tall, thin-faced middle-aged man wearing a Pendleton shirt under a navy cotton sweater, elderly jeans, and black high-top Converse All-Stars. Right. They're everywhere.

The gray car backed out of the parking space. They may be everywhere, but that one, I thought, is the one *I* came with. Damn stick shift, no room to climb into the driver's seat. I flung open the door and ran around the car, then had to run back around and lean in to unlock the driver's door. Around the car again. I crammed myself behind the wheel and began to back out. I had to jam on the brakes to keep from hitting the rattling procession of carts pushed by a figure in a too-large plastic rain poncho. I gritted my teeth.

"This is unbelievable," I fumed aloud. I'd only known Bob for two weeks, but he'd done nothing in that time to indicate he was capable of deserting me in a grocery store parking lot. Even my dead husband

Roger had never done that. Of course I couldn't think of a time Roger and I had gone to a grocery store together. Perhaps only lack of opportunity had kept me from having this delightful experience earlier in life.

The cart parade finally moved past the car. I backed out and zoomed to the entrance to the lot. I saw the Mercedes passing under a streetlight a couple of blocks away. I gunned the engine and the old Honda bucked onto the street. I caught the light at the corner on the yellow and kept the gas pedal pressed to the floor.

Copland's Third Symphony provided grandiose background music to my chase scene. A no-color Pinto pulled out from a side street in front of me, and I stood on the brakes. That's all I needed tonight, to have a Pinto blow up in my face. The Mercedes' red taillights grew smaller and smaller.

I banged on the steering wheel with frustration, uttering phrases unbecoming to a lady, watching for a chance to pass. As soon as I could, I pulled around the plodding Pinto, shifted down to second, and pushed the Civic's four cylinders as hard as they would go. "All right!" I growled as the gap between me and the Mercedes began to close.

Even as I hurtled down Prairie Avenue, I couldn't help wondering if I really was following some other guy while Bob waited back at the grocery store. He'd never leave me the keys again. Supposing we ever went anywhere again.

The Mercedes bounced over the railroad tracks just north of the old Western Electric plant, and as I reached the tracks, a pulsing red light filled the car. I glanced in the rear view mirror. Oh, god, a cop. I looked down at the speedometer and saw the needle hovering near fifty. The speed limit along here was thirty-five. And of course there had been the little matter of passing that Pinto on a two-lane street in town. I looked at the Mercedes' taillights once more and put on my turn signal.

But wait, the cop could catch the Mercedes. I stopped and unclipped my seat belt, shoving open the door. I forgot I hadn't turned off the engine. When I took my foot off the clutch the little car lurched and died. The door swung back and banged my arm. I ignored the pain and scrambled out onto the gravel shoulder. The police car had stopped about fifteen feet behind me. The cop was climbing out. "Officer, there's been a—"

At the sound of my voice he snapped on the large flashlight in his left hand and with his right pulled the heavy revolver holstered at his hip. "Stop right there!" he ordered, pinning me with the beam from the light. I stopped so suddenly that I teetered back and forth. "Get your hands out where I can see them."

I held my hands out to the sides, palms forward and fingers open. "I have to report a kidnap—"

"Turn around slowly and walk back to your car," he said. "Stand by the front wheel and keep your hands in sight."

It's a curious thing about having a gun pointed at you. I felt no trace of the resistance to authority that has occasionally marred my passage through life. I turned and walked to Bob's car.

The officer followed, clicking on the flashlight to inspect the interior. Apparently satisfied by its bareness, he brought the glare of the flashlight around to my face. I blinked and squinted.

"All right, lady, where's the fire?" Stern, gravelly voice. "Don't you know better than to get out of your car when you're stopped by the police?"

"But there's been a—"

"I need your license and vehicle registration."

Maybe it would be faster to give him what he wanted. "They're in the car."

He motioned with the flashlight. "Get in."

He kept the gun in hand as I opened the car door and slipped inside. I grabbed my purse from the floor on the other side. When I turned back and proffered the wallet open to my license, he slid the gun back into its holster. I let out breath I didn't know I'd been holding and then leaned over to reach for the glove box for whatever papers I could find. His reaction was instantaneous.

"Hold it!" he barked. I froze. "What are you reaching for?"

"The registration papers. In the glove box." I risked a glance back at him, but all I could see was the gaping black tunnel of the gun barrel. His middle name must be Quick Draw.

"All right, don't make any sudden moves." He trained the light on the glove box, and with the studied movements of a Bhuto dancer I reached over, clicked open the little door, and brought out the papers I could feel.

When I faced him he holstered his gun once more and picked up my wallet from the ground by his feet. He held the light on my face for a century before moving it to the picture on my license. "Your name is Louisa McGuire?"

"Yes, of course, but—"

He gave a nod, and took the registration.

"Please," I tried again, "you've got to—"

"Your name is not on this registration," he growled. "Is this your car?"

"No! It's Bob's car, and he's—"

"Do you have the owner's permission to drive this vehicle?"

"He was with me and he—"

"He's not with you now."

"That's what I'm trying to tell you! There's been a kidnapping!"

His eyebrows shot up. "What! Your child has been kidnapped?"

"No! Not my child. I don't have a child. I'm talking about Bob."

He glanced at the registration again. "That would be the Robert Richardson who owns this vehicle? Isn't he the guy who's staying in the old stone house out by the river?"

I nodded, remember one reason I had married and gone to live in Seattle, which is about a million people and fifty thousand acres bigger than Willow Falls. Even people you've never met know all your business here.

"What makes you think Mr. Richardson has been kidnapped?

"He got into that Mercedes I was following with a woman in a red suit. You've got to catch them!"

"Where did this take place?"

"At the Food Right. I was waiting in the car and then he came out with this woman and got in her car and—"

He seemed not to be listening to me. He looked at my driver's license again, and back at my face. "Aren't you Kay Chelton's cousin?"

I squinted to read the nametag over the shirt pocket. "E. Johnson." Oh no.

The E stood for Ed, and he and my cousin had a fling a few months ago that had ended badly, at least for her.

"That's right," I said. "But listen, you've got to catch that car and—"

He straightened and looked down Prairie Avenue in the direction I'd been going. It's a straight, flat street and you can see a long way. "What car?"

2

No Mercedes in sight. They could have taken the ramp onto the freeway a few blocks away or turned off anywhere or just gone straight and been out of sight by now. "The car I would have caught if you hadn't stopped me." I sounded cross because I was biting back an epithet. Small town policemen usually don't like to hear women cursing them.

He turned back from gazing down Prairie. "What makes you think he's been kidnapped?"

"Why else would he leave the store with a stranger and drive off in her car?"

"She might not have been a stranger to him. And you did say she was a blonde."

"Okay, but why wouldn't he tell me he was going with her? Bob is not a rude person."

Officer Johnson nodded. "It does seem odd that he would go off and leave his car like that."

Thanks a lot, I thought.

He went on, "Are you sure he didn't look over

and wave or anything?"

"No," I insisted. "I saw them as soon as they came out of the store and watched them walk to her car. Well, I had to wipe some steam off the windows."

"How did she make him go with her? Did you observe any visible coercion?"

"I—I don't know. He came out first with her right behind him. What do you mean by visible coercion? She wasn't pushing him or anything."

"Could she have had a weapon?"

"I think she must have. They were walking really close together."

"But you didn't see a gun or knife or anything."

"Well, no, but she kept her hand in her pocket the whole time, so I think she must have been holding something," I said.

He considered me with narrowed eyes, flexing his shoulders as though they were stiff. "That's a mighty peculiar story."

"Of course it is! That's why I followed them!"

"All right, give me a description of the car and I'll put out an APB on it."

"It's a gray Mercedes, an older one, with the doodad thing on the hood."

"License number?"

I said nothing.

"You didn't get the license number?"

"Well, it was dark and raining and I was still trying to catch them," I hedged. "A Pinto got between us part of the way." No way would I admit that I never once thought of the license number.

He sighed at me. "What about the woman? Can you give me a description of her?"

"She was maybe five foot six. Blonde hair, chin length, a nice figure. She wore a red skirted suit and matching high heels. Very high heels."

"Age?"

"I couldn't tell. She was too far away. She could have been anything from twenty five to fifty."

He chewed on his lower lip. "All right," he said at last. "I'm not going to give you a speeding ticket this time." He proffered my license and the registration papers. "I don't think you need to worry about Mr. Richardson. In my professional opinion a man who drives off in a Mercedes instead of a Honda with a blonde in red high heels is not being kidnapped, but if you get a ransom note or anything you let me know."

"That's your *professional* opinion?" I grabbed my wallet and the registration and flung them on the passenger seat. "I *so* appreciate your professionalism." The rain had stopped, which I regretted. I would have loved for him to get very wet. I restarted the car.

He stepped back. "Mrs. McGuire, drive more carefully than you were when I stopped you. And one more thing..."

I looked at him. Okay, I glared at him.

"How is Kay these days?"

Kay? Bob had been kidnapped and he's asking about Kay? "She's doing very well." I let the unspoken words, "without you," hang in the air between us. I cranked up the window, turned on the left blinker and pulled back onto the road.

I drove a couple of blocks at an ostentatiously moderate pace, trying to bring my angry breathing under control. I felt like I had several heads on my shoulders, all talking at the same time. One said in an annoyingly sensible, know-it-all voice that I should listen to Officer Johnson, there was no reason to worry. People did inexplicable things all the time. Bob could have any number of reasons to ditch me in a grocery store parking lot for a curvy blonde in a red suit. Another voice gave an insinuating laugh and said she could think of at least one. Still another answered back vociferously that Bob was too nice a person to leave me sitting in his car, wondering what had happened to him. And one had some choice words about Officer Johnson and his professional opinion.

I signaled left to go around the block. "All of you, be quiet," I said out loud. "We're going to make sure that we didn't follow some look-alike stranger."

Immediately the know-it-all chimed in. "Don't be ridiculous, you know what Bob looks like. And how many middle aged men in Willow Falls wear canvas high tops?"

"There could be at least two," I answered back. "I haven't known Bob very long, it's the proverbial dark and stormy night, and the windows were all steamed up. This could be just a weird mix up. I might have been wrong about what I saw. Now let me concentrate on driving. I will scream if I am pulled over by the police again tonight, especially if it's the same cop."

3

Bob and I had met two weeks earlier thanks to our cars and our dogs. I had just left my lawyer's office, after dealing with some of the aftermath of my husband's death. The tears I had been blinking back had everything to do with anger and nothing with lost love. Any love I'd had for Roger had died long before he did. I stepped quickly to the tan car at the curb and inserted my key into the lock, but it wouldn't turn. I tried again, with the same result. My tears dried as I scowled at the car, seriously considering kicking it. I heard shouting.

"Hey, get away from my car!"

I looked around and saw a tall man with a short dog hurrying toward me. I was not in the mood to deal with a crazy person. I bent to the task of unlocking the car once more.

"What are you doing to my car?" The voice, closer now, sounded a little winded. I straightened and looked at him, holding my keys defensively in my

13

hand.

"This is my car," I said. I sounded grumpy. "I bought it new in 1989 in Seattle and I've had it ever since." Well, there's a telling detail, said a sarcastic inner voice. That will certainly put him in his place.

He shook his head. "No, sorry, this *is* my car. See, my jacket is on the passenger seat."

I glanced into the car and saw the jacket, and at the same moment remembered I had left my dog Emily Ann in my car. Certainly no sign of her here, unless she had magically morphed into a tan poplin jacket. I looked around and spotted my own car— identical to the one I was trying to unlock— parked two spaces further along, nearly hidden by an enormous SUV. Thousands of tan Honda Civic hatchbacks from the late eighties may still be on the road, since they refuse to die and get great gas mileage to boot. But I'd never before confused mine with another.

"Heavens, you're right, this isn't my car," I exclaimed. I felt my cheeks warming. "Mine is over here—they look the same." I took a couple of steps closer to it and saw Emily Ann wagging at me through the back window.

"Hey, natural mistake," he said, his voice friendlier now. I noticed nice crinkles by his hazel eyes. "Sorry I yelled at you. No way could you see your car behind that behemoth." He was about my age, on the shady side of fifty, with a fair amount of gray in his brown hair. "The first week I had mine, I lost it in a parking lot and it turned out to be hidden by a Subaru."

14

"I know. I once toyed with the idea of carrying a can of helium in the car so I could float a balloon whenever I parked in a big lot."

He nodded. "I tried that for a while, but small children kept stopping and demanding balloons."

A laugh burst out of me. "Oh, that would never do," I said. "Cars this small are considered choking hazards for children under the age of three."

We stepped closer to my car, and this time the key turned in the lock as it had always done before. Emily Ann hopped onto the driver's seat. When I opened the door she descended to the sidewalk and moved to the man's black dog. She ignored me as I grabbed for the leash attached to her collar.

Both tails started wagging. The dogs did their ritual greetings, circling and sniffing. His dog sported a long body, short legs, an exaggerated snout, and long droopy ears, clothed in shiny black hair. "What kind of mix is he?" I couldn't help asking. Dog lovers never can.

"I suspect he's a cross between a black lab and a basset." His voice was a smooth baritone, attractive and curiously soothing. "I always wonder how they know they're both dogs," he added, his eyes on the two animals.

"I know," I agreed, "It must be body language." Certainly the two dogs could not have been more dissimilar physically. Emily Ann is very tall, with a smooth dark gray coat.

They say that people look like their dogs, that we choose pets that reflect us. I think our pets reflect what we find attractive. Emily Ann is a runway-model type—long legs, narrow body, huge eyes and a big smile. Which would also describe this man, who was tall and thin and moved with the same sort of diffident grace. His dog, on the other hand, had that long body and short legs and exhibited not the slightest trace of elegance. And while I'm okay for everyday use, I must admit that I'm long waisted and a bit short legged. My nose is on the small side though, and my ears are *definitely* not droopy.

"I bet he was a really funny puppy," I said, smiling at the sight of his dog stretched out in a play bow with his ears brushing the ground. The bad mood I'd brought out of the lawyer's office had disappeared.

"I imagine he was, but he came to me a gentleman of mature years," Bob said. "I'm Bob Richardson, by the way, and this is Jack." He slung the small backpack he was holding over his shoulder and held out his hand.

"Louisa McGuire," I told him, "and this is Emily Ann." I shook his hand; it was warm and smooth and held mine with just the right amount of pressure.

"And did you get Emily Ann as a pup?"

"No, she spent her early life as a racer. But she didn't make enough money so when she was two her owners turned her over to a rescue group. I've had her about six months."

"Jack's been with me just a few weeks, but I suspect we must have known each other in another life. He felt permanent the first time I met him. You said you bought your car in Seattle, is that where you're from?"

I shook my head. "I grew up here, and moved to Washington when I married. I came back last spring. And you? I don't remember you from high school."

"I've just moved here from High Cross." He looked at his watch. "Two weeks tomorrow. I don't know anyone yet. I bought groceries on Friday so I could chat with the clerks at the grocery store. Pathetic, really. I don't suppose you're actually a grocery clerk in your spare time?"

I shook my head. "Not guilty."

"Any chance you'd take pity and have coffee with me and tell me what I need to know about this place? Do you have time?"

I looked at him. He didn't in any way match my idea of an ax murderer, and he did have a very nice dog. "Well, sure, I don't see why not. Do you know the Bluebird Café around the corner at Third and Maple? They have some outdoor tables where we can have the dogs with us."

"Sounds perfect. What street is this, First? I could toddle a couple of blocks. Do you need to float a balloon or anything?"

"Not this time," I assured him, and turned back to my car. I put the briefcase with its load of unwelcome paperwork behind the seat, slammed the door, and secured it with my key, which turned sweetly in the lock.

4

The Food Right where Bob had left me in his car was an older store that had never been remodeled into a giant warehouse where you needed either hiking boots or roller blades to facilitate your grocery shopping. One of the fluorescent tubes over the bags of charcoal briquettes near the door flickered a bit, almost but not quite keeping time to the luxurious music that washed through the air. It took a moment to recognize it as a string version of the theme song from the old Yogi Bear cartoon show.

I looked down each aisle as I passed, and again as I walked back to the checkout area. It was a slow evening. I saw only two customers in the store: a short woman in her eighties in a pink sweat suit and jogging shoes who swayed to the music as she squinted at the labels on a tuna can, and a young man selecting lettuce, tattoos running out of his sleeveless blue t-shirt

18

to his wrist.

At the front of the store one checkout line was open, inhabited by a clerk in her mid thirties with café au lait skin smoothed over lush curves. Her cheeks were rounded and dimpled, and her eyes nearly disappeared when she smiled at me. She had dozens of long braids that danced as she moved her head. Lounging at the end of the counter was a teenage bag boy. He was so slight I couldn't imagine him lifting full bags into anyone's trunk. He appeared young enough to be working illegally, but was evidently of an age to appreciate the charms of the checker. His eyes were glued to her and while he was not actually drooling, he did appear slightly slack-jawed. But perhaps that was a reaction to the music, which had segued into an elevator version of "Blue Bayou."

The woman gave me her dazzling smile. "Hey, hon," she said, "you need help finding something?"

"Well, sort of," I admitted. "Did either of you notice a tall man in here a little while ago? Brown hair, middle age? He was wearing a plaid shirt and a blue sweater and jeans and high-topped tennis shoes? I was, um, supposed to pick him up and I can't find him."

"Sorry," she said, "I didn't see him. They all run together after a while, you know?"

I nodded. "They do, don't they?" I turned to the boy. "Did you see him?"

He screwed his face up and looked toward the ceiling. "Well, I did see a guy in high tops, which is what I noticed about him? But he wasn't alone, he was with a lady? She was real dressed up and they didn't look like they belonged together? But they went out at the same time so I guess they were."

I thanked them both and left the store. Strains of a relentlessly upbeat-tempo'd "Hey, Jude" followed me into the night. A muddy pickup passed as I stepped off the curb into the parking lot. Bob was not waiting here for me to find him. I could do nothing about him right now. But he had been buying dog food, which meant Jack was hungry. Whatever had happened to Bob, the dog needed to be taken care of. And maybe—why hadn't I thought of this before?—Bob and the blonde had gone to his house. They hadn't been going in that direction, but they could have circled around. They could already be there.

Thickening fog helped the row of dark evergreen trees hide Bob's house from the road. I drove slowly down the long driveway that turned off near the Willow Creek. The only glimmer of light came from the small fixture by the front door and a dim glow through white curtains. No gray Mercedes could be seen.

I'd been here a couple of days earlier to take Bob and Jack to the dog park. In the morning sunshine the place had been charming, but now it seemed positively haunted. I expected to hear movie-soundtrack ooohing sounds from the wisps of fog drifting by the gray stone walls. If it hadn't been for Jack, nothing could have gotten me out of the car. But I heard his absurdly deep bark from inside the house, so I parked as close to the porch as I could, pulled Bob's keys from the ignition, and climbed out.

Bob had a number of keys on his ring. The car key looked like mine, of course, but I had to try several to find the house key. By the time the right one turned in the lock, Jack had stopped barking and was whining and snuffling at the base of the door.

Jack's gladness to see me took the form of circles: he became a whirling dervish of a dog, bucking as he turned. Five times around and then he stopped abruptly, panting and wagging furiously at me.

"Hey, Jack, how's the sweet boy?" I knelt to rumple his baggy coat and receive a small kiss on the earlobe. "Any sign of Bob? No? Well, wait just a minute while I get your leash so we can go out." Oops, I shouldn't have said the O word. He started whirling again.

Bob kept Jack's leash on the knob of the back door. I stepped from the tiny entry into the living room, which was dimly lit by a small lamp on the mantel. Dark blue draperies at the big front window were open, but sheer under-curtains held back the night. I walked past built-in bookcases flanking the fireplace, through an arched doorway to the dining room, and into the kitchen. Another light glowed here, giving enough illumination that I didn't bother to turn on any others. Jack's behavior convinced me that no one else was in the house.

The light came from the hood over the stove. On the counter nearby I saw a red message light blinking on a telephone with a built-in answering machine. Normally I would never listen to someone else's mes-

21

sages. Really. But you could hardly call this evening normal. I punched a button.

The caller had started talking before the beep. "...you're there pick up the phone, I need to talk to you now. Damn. Damn damn damn. Listen, they may have spotted you. I don't know if someone tipped them off or if it was just stupid luck. Be careful. I'll call later." The machine beeped, then gave the time of the call as 6:47.

My heart started beating faster. "Who was that on the phone?" I asked the dog. "Did you recognize the voice?"

He wagged in reply, which was not much help. The message convinced me Bob had not left me marooned on a whim. Maybe it would change Officer Johnson's professional opinion about what had happened. I would call the police station and leave him a message.

I picked up the phone and started to dial 911. Stopped. Was this an emergency? And did 911 calls go to the local station, or somewhere else? Maybe it would be better to call the regular line. I looked around for a phone book. It stood with a short row of neatly arranged cookbooks on the counter, supported by two sturdy bookends decorated with carved wooden owls. I looked up the police station number by the light from the stove hood, and dialed quickly before I lost my nerve.

"Willow Falls Police." I recognized the deep voice that had so annoyed me a short time ago. He hadn't wasted any time getting back to the police station. Did he do everything down there?

"Officer Johnson? This is Louisa McGuire."

"Ah, yes, Mrs. McGuire. How can I help you?" I could hear patience in his voice, which irritated me. A lot.

"I'm at Bob's house. Bob Richardson's. I came to pick up his dog. Jack. So he wouldn't go hungry." I'm babbling, I thought. At least I hadn't burbled anything about not wanting Jack to be forced to pee in the house. Yet.

"Yes?"

"I really do think Bob has been kidnapped. He hasn't come home, and I found a weird message on his phone machine."

"Weird in what way? Can you play it back for me?"

"I don't know," I admitted. I avoid electronic equipment when I can, especially phones. "Will it play while I'm talking on the phone?"

"Push whichever button points to the right." A suspicion of a sigh came over the line.

I squinted at the machine. "Okay, let me try this." I pushed a button.

The machine announced in a metallic voice, "Message erased. There are no further messages."

"Uh oh." I peered more closely at the machine and saw 'Delete' in tiny letters on the button I had pushed.

"What? Mrs. McGuire, did you erase the message?"

"Yes." I really hate telephones.

He breathed at me. "Can you tell me what it

23

said?"

I swallowed hard. "The—the person said that Bob needed to be careful because someone had spotted him."

"Was that the whole message?"

"I think so." I had listened to it only seconds ago but little had lodged in my memory. "They said they'd call again."

"Was the caller a man or a woman?"

"I couldn't tell. It was in that middle register that could be either."

"Did you notice anything about the voice? An accent maybe, or a lisp or something?"

"No, nothing like that."

"I see. So what did you want me to do?"

I felt my jaw tighten. "I want you to look for Bob."

"I see." Didn't the man know any other phrases? "I can't act on a message that doesn't exist. You should make sure the message machine is turned on and go home. Or you could stay in case the caller rings back, or Mr. Richardson returns. Personally, I think you should just go home."

"That's your personal opinion? Not a professional one?"

"In this case it's both. You've had an exciting evening and you should call it a night." He was speaking slowly and evenly.

Did he think I was demented? Perhaps that I had made up this whole unlikely scenario? Crazed widow fakes kidnapping to get attention? The last thing

24

I needed was any more attention of the variety that might include the press; my experience when Roger died was enough to last several lifetimes.

"Thank you, those are no doubt excellent suggestions," I said. "I'm sorry to have bothered you. Good night."

He had more to say. The receiver was squawking as I hung it up. I picked up the answering machine. I wanted very much to smash it on something hard. I swallowed, and held it closer to the light to ascertain that it was still set to take messages. As far as I could tell it was. I put it back where it had been.

"Come on, Jack," I told him, grabbing his leash. "Let's go for a ride. You can have some of Emily Ann's food when we get to my house."

5

I locked the car door as soon as Jack and I were inside. I was in a mood to see phantoms rising out of the swirling fog, crouching just beyond the pool of light that preceded me as I drove back up the drive. I made a left and continued across the river, following the dark curve of the road as it headed west.

"Jack," I said, "what's going on here? Do you know who that blonde woman was?" I glanced over at his attentive face. "You want to know what she looked like? Well, if she were a dog she'd be a standard poodle," I told him. "Groomed for the show ring." I drove for a while, thinking. "You know what seemed really weird? That business of them getting in the same side of the car. Nobody does that anymore. Bucket seats must have ended that. I haven't seen anyone do that since I was about seventeen years old and we know how long that's been."

Jack cocked his head to one side as though to

ask, how long?

"Just do the math yourself," I told him tartly. Not that I cared if anyone knew my age, let alone a dog, but I didn't think *I* could do the math and drive at the same time, at least not tonight. "That car must have been old enough to have bench seats. It really was a classic."

I glanced in the rear view mirror. Headlights. They felt too close. I slowed to make a right turn, then speeded up. The headlights maintained the same distance. "How long has that car been behind us?" I asked Jack. I told myself it was ridiculous to be worried, but at the next intersection I made another right turn, and so did the other car. I drove a few blocks and made a quick left into a residential area and floored the accelerator. I'd gone only half a block when a car turned from the street I'd been on.

Was I being followed, or was it a coincidence? A couple of random turns in this neighborhood of curving streets should tell me. I signaled and turned right. Damn it, I thought, stop with the signaling. I'd been law abiding for too long, no matter what Officer Johnson might think. I curled around the next bend before I saw if the other car turned or not.

In the middle of the block I noticed a house that had no lights on. I pulled into the driveway and doused my lights, hoping that no one was home to call the cops or get out the tea and cookies. I slid down in my seat so that my head was level with the headrest. Jack whined and nudged his short front legs into my lap, and I hugged him hard as we cowered in the dark.

27

My heart had time for only three or four quick thuds before headlights appeared at the end of the block and swung around the corner. As the car accelerated, I sat still as any cornered prey, hoping for invisibility. It worked. The other car swept past and disappeared around the next corner. It was black or some other dark color. The driver was alone in the vehicle. In a few seconds it was gone.

I didn't waste any time. I started Bob's car and rolled back into the street, using gears instead of brakes to slow my backward movement. I left the headlights off until I'd gone nearly a block. The street remained deserted behind me.

"Don't worry, Jack, everything's going to be okay," I assured him—and myself—as I retraced my turns and headed for home again. I drove a little over the speed limit, and no headlights stayed in my rearview mirror for more than a few blocks. And no one pulled me over for speeding.

Ten minutes later I was home. As I pulled into my drive, I reached up to the passenger-side visor to press the button on the remote control for the garage door. A rattle of panic ran through me when it wasn't I couldn't feel it. It took a moment to remember I wasn't in my own car. I'd have to go through the house to raise the garage door to park Bob's car inside.

I fumbled in my purse for my own keys and led Jack to the porch. He graciously allowed me to enter first and bounced in behind me. Across the living room, Emily Ann flowed off the couch and stretched, her thin tail waving. She and Jack touched noses in greeting before she came to lean against me so I could rub her chest.

"Hey, sweet pup," I said, "were you a good girl?" She was always a good girl, so this was a mere formality. I padded into the kitchen. A bottle of merlot sat on the counter. I wrenched the cork out of the bottle and poured myself a glass. "Did you take any messages?" I said to Emily Ann, who had followed me. "I'd better check."

I keep only one phone in the house, in the bedroom, and the dogs jostled at my heels as I traipsed down the hall. The bedroom was in darkness, but no red message light blinked. Emily Ann had taken no calls. Bob had not phoned to tell me he'd met someone else and been swept off his feet, or that the woman in red wanted a ransom. I took a swig of my wine, and looked down at the dogs. Jack sat in front of me and looked up beseechingly, the tip of his tail moving on the floor.

"Oh. Yes. Your dinner," I said. Emily Ann, hearing a word related to food, wagged as well. "You've had yours, you opportunist," I told her. We trailed back to the kitchen, where I grabbed a cake pan from a lower cabinet. I went to the garage where I kept the bin of dog food and scooped some into the pan, grabbing a handful for Emily Ann as well.

Being in the garage reminded me that Bob's car was still sitting in my drive. I reached for the button to open the garage door, but my hands were full of dog food. First things first. I went back to the kitchen, settled Jack with his dinner, and fed Emily Ann's snack to her piece by piece as I drank a couple more sips of wine.

One thing about feeding dogs, it's not a time-consuming occupation. In less than two minutes the food was gone, and I let both dogs into the back yard. Another couple of minutes and they were back, jostling each other for my attention. I patted them both, took one more sip of wine, and picked up Bob's keys so I could bring in his car.

That's when the phone rang.

6

"Maybe it's Bob," I said to the dogs. They heard the excitement in my voice as an invitation to play and began to tussle with each other. I had to push around them, and before I reached the bedroom, the machine beeped to signal that the outgoing message was over.

"Hey! Lou! Pick up the phone! I know you're home, you know I know it, you know you can't hide from—"

I grabbed the receiver. "Kay," I said to my cousin, "you're going to wake my neighbors."

She lowered her voice a trifle. "Yeah, well, they sleep too much anyway. Did you and Bob have fun tonight?"

"He—"

"Anything interesting happen? Did you kiss him yet?"

"No, he—"

"Just because your husband was a lying sleaze-

31

bag son of a bitch doesn't mean all men are," the font of wisdom on the other end of the line continued.

"We don't have a kissing kind of relationship, and besides—"

"I like Bob, and obviously he likes you, even though you are reluctant about the kissing, which is probably only natural after Roger, and—"

"I think he's been kidnapped," I butted in. My legs gave way and I sat down heavily on the edge of the bed. There was a pause, then a snort of laughter.

"That is good," Kay chuckled. "Space aliens?"

"No. Woman in red, at the grocery store."

Another pause, longer this time. "Louisa, what are you talking about?"

I took a deep breath. "Bob and I went out to dinner this evening, and afterward he went into the grocery store to get some dog food while I waited in the car because it was raining and I wore my velveteen sneakers and he came out with a woman and got into her car and they drove away and I tried to follow but I lost them."

"Whoa, whoa, wait a minute! Slow down. You're not making any sense. You and Bob went to dinner—"

"Right."

"And then you went to a grocery store? He really knows how to show you a good time, doesn't he?"

"Kay," I flared, sitting up straighter, "the Food Right was on the way to my house and he needed to get food for Jack. He said he was going to run in for a minute and come right back out."

Jack must have heard his name. He appeared

in front of me and leaned heavily against my legs.

"Okay, okay. Whatever. He ran in for dog food and came right back out, but he came out with another woman?"

"Yes. And he didn't have any dog food." I leaned over and patted Jack's head.

"I hate to say it but that is pretty damned tacky." I could tell from her voice that she was wrinkling her nose the way she does when she doesn't like something. An image of her in first grade faced with a slimy wad of canned spinach on her lunch plate swam up from my memory.

"It would be more than tacky if he did it on purpose." I sat back up. "And I suppose he could have. After all, Roger—"

"Don't even go there," she snapped. "I forbid you to ever compare Bob with Roger, even if Bob did leave you at the Food Right. I mean, ditching you at the store is nothing compared to—"

"Yes, yes, okay," I interrupted in turn, waving my free hand. "You're right, Roger was far beyond tacky. But Kay, I don't think he did it on purpose. Bob, I mean. The woman was practically glued to his side, and I think she had a gun or a knife or something."

"What!"

"Well, I couldn't really see her hands," I admitted. "She was partly behind Bob and she kept one hand in her jacket pocket. But why else would he just walk off with someone and not even look my way?" I chewed my lower lip as I pictured the scene again. "He walked...I don't know, sort of stiffly. Tense. Not talking and laughing together like you would if you've just picked someone up. Or met someone you know. She made him unlock the car door. As though she had to keep her eyes on him the whole time. And they both got in the passenger side, and he slid over behind the wheel to drive."

"Wouldn't the transmission get in the way?" she asked.

"The car had a bench seat. I think. It was an old car. A gray Mercedes with the silver thingie on the hood."

"So at least he went off with someone who had a cool car."

"I don't think Bob cares all that much about cool cars," I said, annoyed.

"True, look what he drives. And don't get all huffy at me. I know it's just like yours. So what did this woman look like, anyway?"

I described the woman and her red suit and heels.

"Weird outfit for a grocery store," my cousin said. "Maybe she just ran in for something too and saw Bob and—"

"Decided he was on her take-out menu for tonight?"

"Maybe they knew each other."

"It's possible. I just don't know. Anyway, they drove off, and I followed them—"

"He left his keys? He must have, I can't see you hotwiring a car."

"Yes, he left his keys. So I could listen to the

radio. And I bet you can't hotwire one either. Anyway I followed, and a Pinto pulled out in front of me and they were getting further away, so I passed it and I was probably speeding a little, because a cop pulled me over and I lost them."

A little silence played along the line. "A cop?"

"Yes."

"Not..."

"Yes."

"Did he know who you were?"

"You mean that I'm your cousin? Oh yes."

"Did he manage to piss you off?"

"Yes."

"That figures. What did he do?"

"You mean aside from not listening to me until the Mercedes had disappeared from sight, and telling me that in his professional opinion it made perfect sense for a man to go off in a Mercedes instead of a Honda, especially with a blonde involved? Other than that he pretty much told me to drive carefully and call him if I got a ransom note."

"Goddammit!" she snarled. I knew she had bounced to the edge of whatever she was sitting on. "How dare he talk to my cousin like that! This is *so* typical. What a lug he is!"

"Thanks, Kay." I was warmed by her partisanship. "But to be fair, I was telling him a really weird story, I was driving someone else's car, and I was speeding. Not a whole lot, it isn't easy to speed seriously in an eighty-nine Civic, but still. Anyway, after he let me go, I went back to the store to look for Bob.

35

Just in case it hadn't really been him. But he wasn't there. So I went to his house to get Jack."

"No sign of Bob?"

"No, but I found a phone message. I saw the machine blinking and thought maybe he'd called and maybe I should listen—" I realized I was twisting the phone cord around my finger and stopped.

"Anyone would have done the same," she assured me. "What was the message?"

"Someone telling Bob that he'd been found and should be careful. That was pretty much it."

"Did you take the tape with you?"

"No, I—"

"That's what they always do in the movies."

"Yeah, well, in the movies they have phone machines with tapes in them. This was the digital kind that doesn't use a tape. But I thought the police should know about it so I called them."

"Did Kerry Sue Maddock answer the phone? I swear that is the stupidest woman in town."

"No, your friend Ed had already made it back to the station."

"Uh oh. What happened?"

"He asked me to play the message for him."

"Then what did he say?"

"Before I managed to erase the message or after?" I hedged. I shrugged my shoulders to release some tension.

"Louisa! You *erased* it?" She sounded like she was choking back a laugh. "Of course you did. Why do I even ask?" My track record with electronics is not outstanding. "Then what?"

"He told me either to wait and see if they called again, or go home. He sounded like he was tiptoeing around a nut case. I'm sure he thought I'd made the whole thing up. So I hung up and came home. What did you tell him about me, anyway?"

"Nothing."

"Nothing? You never said you had a cousin in Seattle?"

"Of course I told him *that*. But we haven't spoken to each other for months, so he wouldn't know about your more recent history, or rather Roger's, if that's what's worrying you. *I* certainly didn't tell him anything about it."

"Kay, everyone in the world knows about all that."

"They do not! Geez, get over it!"

"Easy for you to say. But anyway, I got Jack and started home, and someone was driving close behind me soon after I left Bob's place, and I made a bunch of turns and a car was always behind me. I finally shook it off and came home."

Now that I'd narrated this madness to another person I felt impossibly tired. I wanted to let my lead-weighted bones collapse on the bed and sleep until all this—whatever it was—was over. Stress takes me that way.

"Louisa, what have you gotten yourself into? This whole thing is so weird," Kay said. "It will probably turn out to have a mundane explanation, but it *is* weird."

"No kidding," I agreed. "Do you think I should call Officer Johnson again?"

"It's actually Chief Johnson," she said.

"He's the *chief?* You never said you were dating the chief of police. What was he doing out chasing speeders? Shouldn't he have been at the station telling everyone else what to do?"

"Hey, it's a small town, they all do everything."

"Well, anyway, should I tell him about being followed? He already thinks I'm insane. Maybe I should call someone else, the county sheriff or the FBI or something."

She snorted. "Louisa! The *FBI?* By the time they figure out where Willow Falls is, Bob could be back again." Silence. I knew she was rubbing the bridge of her nose as she thought. "Listen, don't call anyone else tonight. In movies a person always has to be missing for twenty four hours before they'll start looking for them."

"You think?" I asked, wanting to believe her. "But what if I delay and something happens to him?"

"Something's already happened to him," she pointed out. "But you have no idea if he went with that woman voluntarily. I know you think he didn't, but we can't be sure."

"Not being sure is making me nuts. If I knew for certain that he'd ditched me I could just get really mad, or if he was kidnapped I could make someone look for him. As it is I can't do anything." I sighed and shifted restlessly on the bed, then saw that I was still holding Bob's keys. "Listen, I just remembered, I left

38

Bob's car in the driveway and I want to move it into the garage."

"All right, sweetie, you move the car in and get some sleep. Will you be okay by yourself? Do you want me to come over?"

"I'll be okay," I assured her. "After all, Emily Ann and Jack are here."

"No problem then." I could hear a grin in her voice. "No harm can come to you with those two in the house. I'll be in the store early tomorrow if you need me. Ambrose is having a piece picked up practically at dawn."

"Did you need me to work tomorrow?"

"No, that's okay. But if Bob's not back by tomorrow afternoon we will have to decide who to report his disappearance to. Call me immediately if you hear from him. *When* you hear from him."

I hung up the phone and slumped on the edge of the bed. I knew if I let myself lie down, even for a second, I'd never get up again that night. Still, I was about to fall back onto the covers when I realized both dogs had sneaked up behind me and were curled on the bed flank to flank. I didn't have the heart to disturb them. I forced myself to my feet and out to the garage. My car was far enough to the side to be able to park the other, so I pressed the doorbell-like button that opens the garage door.

The door started up and the overhead light came on. Too late, I realized I was spotlighted for anyone who might be outside. I felt I was in one of those dreams where you're on stage and don't know what the play is, let alone what your lines might be. What if someone had followed me home, and here I was armed only with bunch of keys? I didn't even have the dogs to protect me, assuming that their friendly overtures to everyone they met would be any protection.

But when the door was up, no one was in sight. I quickly moved the Honda inside beside its twin, pressed the button again, and went back into the house. The damp night air, not to mention the fear I'd felt when I stepped out into it, had revived me. I was wide awake again. I sat at the kitchen table to finish my glass of wine, hoping it would lull me enough to bring sleep.

The only sounds were the ticking of the Seth Thomas clock on the mantel and its chime on the quarter hour, and the low hum of the refrigerator. I rolled the stem of the wine glass around in my fingers as I thought of this evening. It struck me that Bob was a watchful person, always looking around him when he was out in public.

I heard a thump from the bedroom. Nails clicked on the hardwood floor of the hall. Jack appeared in front of me.

"Jack," I said to him, "I'm confused. Bob's the first guy I've gone out with since my husband died, and I was married for a long time, but I don't recall having the person you're with being swept away by a woman in red as part of the conventional dating ritual. Of course, everyone says things have changed since the last time I did any of this, but still, this seems somewhat out of the norm."

Jack yawned.

"And of course it had to be a blonde. My recent experience with blondes has not been good. I know of one in Seattle...no, you're too young for that story."

Jack gave himself a mighty shake, so that his ears made a leathery flapping sound and his lips flew up to expose his shining teeth. He turned and started toward the bedroom, looking over his shoulder at me.

"You're right," I said. "Let's call it a day."

I leaned over to untie my shoes. They were soaked through and the pattern of silver moons and stars barely showed through the smears of mud. I put them in the trash and went to bed.

7

I expected to stare into the dark for most of the night; that single glass of wine was not enough to have a soporific effect. But Jack's presence helped; he's a snuggly dog. He pressed his long back against my side, and his warmth spread into me. Emily Ann lay crossways near the top of the bed with her chin three inches from my shoulder. I was asleep in two minutes.

The red numbers on the digital clock glowed 5:37 when my eyes unglued the next morning. I tried to pull the quilt a little higher on my shoulder but it wouldn't budge. Jack was still snoring beside me, and for a moment I had no idea what he was doing in my bed. Then I remembered Bob getting into a Mercedes with an unknown blonde and driving away; Chief Johnson who thought I was insane; ominous phone messages and hiding in a stranger's driveway to elude a following car—if Jack had not been at my side I would have been sure it was all a dream.

I untangled myself from the heap that the two

dogs and I had become, sat up and yawned. Jack jumped off the foot of the bed and did his stretches, and wagged his way to me. "You want to go out?" I asked him. The rate of wagging increased. "How about you?" I asked Emily Ann, who was still curled on her side in the middle of the bed. She gave me an affronted glance and turned over. "Hang on a minute," I told Jack. A trip to the bathroom and a quick swipe over my teeth with a wet but paste-less toothbrush sufficed.

Jack danced me down the hall and just before we reached the kitchen I heard Emily Ann thumping down from the bed. I let them out the back door and headed for the fridge.

Orange juice was the first item on the agenda. Real orange juice is a food group unto itself. When they talk about the nectar and ambrosia of the gods, this has to be the nectar. Most mornings I cut Valencias or navels and use a juicer to squeeze a big glass. Today I couldn't be bothered. I poured from the pitcher of the frozen stuff I keep mixed up for doses during the day.

I heard the dogs jostling each other at the back door and let them in, glancing at the still dark sky. The rain clouds had cleared, though in October the weather can jump from sun to rain in no time. I carried my glass of juice back to the bedroom, where I pulled on jeans and a blue sweatshirt.

"Jack," I said, "I don't know where to even start looking for Bob. You don't have any ideas, do you?" His wagging tail indicated that he had lots of ideas but none on this subject. "Geez, he's the only person I know besides me who doesn't carry around a cell phone." I thought about calling Bob's house, but I'd had strict training from my mother that phone calls could not be made before eight in the morning or after ten at night. I harbored irrational fears that if I broke that rule I would inevitably call a wrong number and wake some total stranger.

Where could someone look for information about me if I had disappeared? They would only have to ask Kay, who knew practically everything about me. Bob had only lived here a matter of weeks. But he'd had a whole life in High Cross before he moved here. He must have had friends, and he'd told me he was a freelance writer so he would need contacts to do that.

"I know," I said. Both dogs pricked their ears at me. "Writers use computers. Let's go look at Bob's and see if it gives us anything useful."

I ran a brush through my hair before leading the dogs back to the kitchen. I scooped dog food into a couple of bowls, and while Emily Ann and Jack scarfed that down I slipped my wallet into a fanny pack and strapped it on. In a few minutes we were all bundled into my car, with the garage door closing on Bob's vehicle, now safely hidden from view.

Streaks of pink clouds lit up the eastern sky, while half a moon lingered above the opposite horizon. The lacy forms of half-bare trees shivered in a dawn breeze. Only a few other cars were out this early, dark anonymous shapes behind their glowing headlights.

I passed the turn for Maple Street and Kay's store. Though she's my first cousin, a lot of people assume we're sisters. We obviously come from the same gene pool. Our fathers were brothers, and we look more alike than they did.

During the time I lived in Seattle, I gave up on the idea of ever being a thin person, and Kay kept dieting year after year. Thirty years later we have basically the same body. I wear my hair short and she has shoulder length waves; under the warm honey color she uses it's the same shade of ashy brown streaked with gray as mine. I'm taller by three inches, and ten months older, and when we argue she nearly always wins.

My parents took every opportunity throughout my childhood to drop me off to play with my little cousin. I always wanted her parents instead of mine. My Aunt Poppy and Uncle Bill were wonderful, cheerful and hardworking. And they adored their daughter; the three of them did everything together. Looking back, I think Kay should have been a lot more spoiled than she was, but Poppy especially didn't let her get away with much.

My parents existed only for each other. I spent my early years hearing people sigh over their great love story, telling me how inspiring it was to see two people who were so much in love. Maybe it's just my faulty memory, but I can hardly recall anyone ever speaking of them without using the word love.

One day when I was nine or ten, I was at Kay's house. We'd been outdoors playing and had argued over something, so I had come inside to read. I always brought along a library book, and had settled down quietly in a nook in the upstairs hall with *The Mystery on the Old Island*. The phone rang downstairs and my aunt answered it. "Of course," I heard her say, "you know we love having her. Sure. All right, about 8:30." She hung up the phone and her footsteps clicked across the wood floor of the hall, back into the living room where she'd been reading the morning paper with Uncle Bill.

"That was Eloise," I heard her report. A crisp rustle of newsprint made me sit up straighter to listen. Eloise was my mother.

"And I suppose they want her to spend the night."

"Of course."

Silence hovered in the air like dust motes in a beam of light. Then my uncle said, "You know, I would buy into this great love story of theirs a lot more if they managed to divert just a little affection to their daughter."

I sat very still in my nook with my book open on my lap, several thoughts chasing around in my head. I must be pretty unlovable if my own parents didn't love me, but my aunt and uncle did, so I couldn't be completely awful. But clearer than that was a feeling almost of satisfaction, that my uncle had voiced my own unspoken thoughts. Someone else had noticed what I thought only I had seen, and that meant that it was real.

The turn for Bob's driveway brought me back to

the present. The scene was completely different from the previous night: instead of darkness and fog, a wind high up blew broken clouds across the increasingly light sky. The gray stone of the little house gleamed silver in the dawn light.

I parked the car in front of the house, leaving my keys in the ignition and clutching Bob's set. I kept Emily Ann's leash in my hand as we walked to the house, but I didn't bother with Jack's. I didn't want her to take off into the woods after some real or imagined prey, but he was unlikely leave us. This time I picked the right key for the front door the first time, and the three of us stepped into the silent house. Emily Ann went straight to the sofa and curled up on it, trailing her blue leash.

I called out a tentative, "Hello? Bob?" but I wasn't surprised when no one answered. Everything looked the same as last night, and the light still burned in the kitchen. After only one night's abandonment the house felt cold and unused.

Bob's home was sparsely equipped with basic middle-American stuff: a sofa and matching chair with a coffee table between them in the living room; round maple table with four chairs in the dining room. Bob had said that he'd rented the place furnished. He had added little of a personal nature to the front part of the house, no family photos or collections or books. With the exception of some short black dog hairs on the seat of the chair, everything was tidy.

The white sheers at the big front window became see-through in the growing daylight. I stood in the living room staring blankly past them to the grassy front yard and my car parked in the drive until Jack poked me with his cold nose.

"What?" I asked him. "All right, I'm back from Lala Land."

The voices in my head had evidently been conversing, and now the sensible one said, "Go on, look for his computer."

The prissy one decided to be scandalized. "Invading his privacy? You still aren't sure if he was really kidnapped."

"Just take a look and if it's too private turn it off again. But if we find a file named 'Open this if I'm kidnapped by a woman in a red suit' go ahead and read it."

The most sardonic voice said, "Just don't erase anything."

"Okay, okay," I said out loud. Jack wagged in response. "Where's the computer, boy?" He wagged again but didn't move. Evidently I'd have to find it myself.

With Jack at my heels I started down the short hall. The first door on the left opened into a compact bathroom, tiled in a Fifties pink with gray trim. I leaned in to flip on the light. Gray towels hung neatly over a wooden bar and shaving equipment marched in a line along the edge of the sink. I was tempted by the medicine cabinet but it seemed an unlikely place for a computer. Still, maybe I'd find prescription bottles that might tell me something. I pulled open the mirrored door and looked with disappointment at bare

48

shelves that held only a bottle of ibuprofen and a box of Band-Aids.

Further along the hall I found a small bedroom furnished with a twin bed in the corner, neatly made up with white sheets and a brown wool blanket. A faded depiction of Little Bo Peep and her peripatetic sheep decorated the pillowcase. A small brown student type desk stood in front of the window, but no computer graced its bare surface. I pulled open the single drawer. Inside was a pad of steno paper, a box of envelopes and a couple of pencils. The small closet was completely empty, not even a wire hanger dangling from the rod.

The other bedroom was equally neat and impersonal, except for a rather nice old quilt in a flying geese pattern spread over the double bed. Four pillows in plain white cotton covers rested on top of the quilt. A couple of library books—the latest by Dean Koontz and an early Dick Francis—inhabited the bedside table. I opened the closet door, and had to lean against the door frame as I took in Bob's scent from his collected clothing. Jack touched the back of my leg with his nose.

"I'm scared, Jack," I told him. "Do you think I was right to follow Kay's advice last night and not call anyone else?" Another thought struck me. "Maybe *Bob* wouldn't have wanted me to call the police. He could have all kinds of reasons to go off with that woman. He said he's a writer. Maybe she's part of a story. Or maybe *he's* done something awful." I shook my head. This was as hard for me to believe as a kidnapping.

A shelf over the closet rod was slightly too high for me to see. I gave as much of a hop as my age and body type would allow. It wasn't much of a look but unless Bob had a computer as thin as a piece of typing paper, nothing was up there.

I turned to the mahogany chest of drawers between the room's two windows. One drawer was occupied by boxers and tee shirts, another with a couple of sweaters, and the rest were empty. On its well polished top a white milk glass dish held forty-seven cents in change and a folded Kleenex. A little carved wooden box boasted several miscellaneous items—two collar stays, some stray keys, three English coins, a couple of two-cent stamps, a watch band with no watch, and a folded piece of paper that turned out to be the instructions for his phone machine.

"Too bad I didn't find this last night before I called Officer Ed," I said to Jack, who panted in agreement. "Doesn't Bob *have* a computer?" I asked the dog. "How can he write? If he has a laptop, it certainly wasn't with him last night when he drove off with that women. And it's not in his car. Come on, maybe it's in the kitchen."

8

Two Weeks Earlier

Bob and the dogs and I turned the corner from First onto Maple. "This is nice," Bob said looking around. "I used to hear about this place when I lived in High Cross."

The autumn sun mellowed the facades of restored two-story buildings, most built in the late nineteenth century of brick and native stone. A variety of upscale shops and restaurants, including my cousin's antique store, attracted clusters of well-dressed women and an occasional man, even on a weekday morning in October.

"You haven't been here before?" I asked. He shook his head. "It used to be pretty depressing, back in the Sixties and Seventies."

Bob paused in front of the store that specializes

in vintage radios. His gaze lingered on a beautiful floor model from the Forties, with rounded edges and Bakelite knobs. "I remember seeing an article in—was it *Newsweek*? I guess I thought anything this popular would be tacky." He laughed. "I'm putting my foot in my mouth, I'd better be quiet."

We moved on. Emily Ann and Jack walked side by side in front of us, getting smiles from almost everyone we passed.

"I thought so too," I said. "I have deeply rooted notions about anything touristy. But when I moved back here I found it's...maybe homey is the word."

We crossed Second and passed the toy store with the old Lionel train in the window, then Bob paused once more to study the yarn shop display, a tangle of silks artfully arranged around a toy tiger kitten.

That's when I heard a voice calling my name.

"Louisa! Oh, LEW-EEEE-SA! Is that you?"

I froze, unable to believe my ears. Moving two thousand miles to a small Midwestern town had not been enough. I looked over my shoulder and saw a tall, broad shouldered woman crossing the street, carefully highlighted and tousled hair gleaming in the morning sun. Her brown slacks and matching shirt looked expensive, and a dramatic ankle length duster of heavy cream silk flapped around her.

"Oh. My. God." I muttered. As she drew near, I bared my teeth in what the charitable might mistake for a smile. Bob looked back and forth between us with an interested expression.

The woman stopped in front of us, giving Bob a thorough inspection before focusing on me. She ignored the dogs. "I *thought* that was you." Her voice was nearly as loud as when she was shouting across the street. "So this is where you ended up, or are you visiting too? *And*, I see, not alone. Have you remarried *already*?" She cocked her head and raised her brows at Bob.

As the dogs sat down side-by-side and peered up at our faces, I pried my stiff jaws apart to make some sort of answer. But Bob was ahead of me.

"No, no," he said in bluff and reassuring tones, "Louisa and I are just old friends. She grew up here, you know. I'm Bob Richardson." He stuck out his hand and pumped hers up and down.

"Um, Bob, this is Doris Carter," I managed, "who used to work with my husband."

"Yes, poor Roger," she sighed. She slowly shook her head and closed her eyes, the picture of sadness. "Such a tragic loss, though given the circumstances I don't suppose *you* felt it as much as the rest of us." She pressed her right hand against her chest where her heart would be if she had one.

My cheeks flamed as I tried to find something to say, something I could say aloud, since "you vicious harridan, I wish you would spontaneously combust" didn't seem quite tactful. But again, Bob stepped in.

"You know, one of the things I have always admired about Louisa is her ability to keep her private feelings private," he said, a friendly smile relentlessly in place. Before Doris could react, he went on, "And are you staying in the area? It's a great time of year for a visit, isn't it?"

"Why, yes, I got a chance to combine business and pleasure," she told him, and everyone else within a block who was not stone deaf. "I have a conference in St. Louis on Thursday, so I decided to spend a few days checking out the shopping here. I've heard so much about it. I bought a little vacation home on Whidbey Island recently and it needs just everything."

"Well, you've certainly come to the right place," he told her confidently. "Don't miss the shop with the antique linens, and OKay Antiques is rather special too. Now, if you'll excuse us, these dogs are getting restless." He continued to smile pleasantly, took me by the elbow to get me moving, and shook his obviously placid dog's leash. "Come on, Jack, let's get that cookie we promised you." And we moved down the street away from Doris.

When we were far enough away not to be overheard, Bob looked down at me with a rueful expression. "I'm sorry," he said, "that was really pushy of me, but bullies annoy me. She is a bully, isn't she? I hope I didn't read her wrong. Tell me she's not your oldest friend."

A little laugh forced its way out of me. "She's absolutely a bully, and no friend at all. I always think next time I'll stand up to her, but I'm so amazed at what she's willing to say that I stand gaping like an idiot."

"Not at all. The rude have a serious advantage." His smile was slightly wicked. "But being politely rude back can be fun."

At the Bluebird Café I reached for the gate that led into the patio, but Bob already held it open. I walked over to the door into the café. The window in the upper half framed the picture of a waitress pouring coffee into a heavy china mug for a woman with curly black hair and bright cheeks, sitting at the counter. I tapped on the glass, and they both looked around and waved. Raising my hand in greeting, I pointed toward the patio tables. The waitress nodded back at me.

Pantomime over, I turned back to Bob. "How about over here?" I twitched Emily Ann's leash, and we went to a table in the back corner. I was going to sit in the chair facing the street, but Bob pulled out the one on the other side of the table with a little gesture. I settled myself in it and smiled at him, enjoying the contrast between his courtly manners and the way Roger had ignored me when we were in public together. Bob hung his pack from the back of the other chair and sat, gazing over my shoulder toward the street. Emily Ann settled in the shade of the large green market umbrella by my chair. Jack looked around, sniffing the air.

"Jack, lay down," Bob said, and the dog obligingly went under the table, giving a little grunt as he flopped on the brick floor.

I knew that by lunchtime the place would be full, but now only one other table was occupied. A bearded man with fluffy red hair tonsured around a shining bald spot read the High Cross newspaper, sipping from a mug.

"You know, you were amazing. Are you an actor?" I asked Bob. "You came up with that stuff so quickly, it was like watching improvisational theater. I thought you'd never been down here before."

"I haven't, but I could see the stores across the street from where we were standing. I thought it might get her moving. I can't say I immediately warmed to her."

"She's horrible, and she's horrible on purpose. And she's a lawyer, so she's also horrible by profession. I can't believe she's here. I thought I'd never have to see her again. If she really does go into OKay Antiques we'll have to fumigate, or have an exorcism."

"You know the place?"

"It belongs to my cousin. Kay. I work for her part time."

"Does Kay know Doris?"

"I'm sure she'll recognize her from my husband's funeral, but I don't think they spoke to one another. Doris doesn't notice people as individuals unless they are clients."

"I gathered from what she said that you're a widow. I'm sorry," he said simply.

"Um, thanks." Several voices erupted in my head, the haughty one insisting that my private business was my private business, and another reminding me that I didn't want to think about Roger, let alone speak of him. Still another said Bob saved you from Doris, you owe him some sort of explanation. Just keep it light. "It was kind of—ugly. We had just split

56

up when he died."

I bit my lip to prevent more from spilling out. The arrival of Cleta, the waitress, saved me. Her graying hair towered above her in a beehive, and her outfit of classic shirtwaist dress and little apron was complemented by the enormous cross trainers on her feet. "Mornin', Louisa," she greeted me, looking with interest at Bob. "How you doin' on this beautiful day?"

Too late I realized that coming here might have been a bad idea. Not that Cleta is a gossip, but Maple Street is a tight little community, and everyone knows everyone else's business. No doubt word had already started to travel that I was sitting on the patio at the Bluebird with a strange man and his dog. When I'd peeked inside from the patio, Cleta had been pouring coffee for Eileen, who owns Trellis Island, the garden-art store. I knew that two minutes after she downed the contents of that mug, she would be in my cousin's shop saying, "Kay, you'll never guess who I just saw at the café."

I shrugged mentally and smiled up at Cleta. "Hey, Cleta," I answered. "I'm good. This is Bob and his dog Jack. They're new in town and I wanted them to get off on the right foot café-wise."

"Nice to meetcha," Cleta nodded at Bob, and looked around for Jack. He emerged from under the table, wagging. "And you must be Jack," Cleta said. He wagged harder. "Well, you be a good boy and I'll bring you a cookie."

She turned back to Bob and me. "So what'll it be? Dog biscuits all around, or do y'all want something less crunchy?" A stub of pencil hovered over her order pad, which was solely for the convenience of the kitchen since Cleta never forgot anything.

"I want a pot of Earl Gray, hot," I told her.

She grinned at my Star Trek reference. "You got it, Captain."

"And one of Dorothy's cinnamon rolls," I added.

"Coffee for me, and a cinnamon roll sounds great," Bob said.

"All righty then," Cleta said, and went to get our food.

Jack followed her for a couple of steps. "Here, boy," Bob said, and he turned back to lie by Bob's chair.

I looked at Bob and tried to conjure up some normal, socially acceptable remark. "How about you? Are you married?" *That's* subtle, said one of my mental voices. Go ahead and cut right to the chase.

He looked rueful. "I was, several years ago, but my wife decided a struggling writer wasn't as good a bet as an insurance actuarial. I haven't been brave enough to try it again."

Instant alarms went off in my head. "You're a writer? A reporter?" I hoped my voice sounded normal and only mildly interested.

"Nothing that exciting. I do technical manuals and the occasional magazine piece."

"So no newspaper stuff?" If he was a reporter, I thought, I'd have to be careful. I'd learned from the publicity surrounding my husband's death that the most innocuous utterance could become something

58

quite different when quoted out of context on the front page of a newspaper.

"Not really, just any kind of freelance I can sell. You said you work for your cousin in her antique store?"

"Yes, part time. I mind the store when she needs to be somewhere else, and help her move stuff around, and buy stuff at garage sales, which is fun. What kind of magazine pieces have you done?"

"Oh, uh, usually for trade publications. You know, the latest on potato blight for a farmers' co-op newsletter, how technology is changing the way pipelines are riveted together."

"People really read about that stuff?"

"Only potato farmers and pipeline riveters. I never seem to do anything any normal person would want to know about."

"I'm not sure how much normality I can claim, but I admit I've never read anything on those topics."

"Did you work in an antique store in Seattle?"

I shook my head. "I was the personnel, excuse me, human resources manager for a computer firm. You know, I never liked that phrase. Human resources. Made me feel like I was involved in a cover up for something illegal."

Bob chuckled. "Yeah, people as products. Maybe I could get an article out of that for some HR newsletter. So did you up and quit your job to move back here?"

"No, shortly before my husband died the company went belly up. And both my parents died within a few weeks of each other, and I inherited their house. So I moved back to Willow Falls."

"That's rough."

I shrugged. "For a while I made my way through the entire top half of that chart that assigns numerical values to life events so you can rate exactly how stressed out you are."

Bob nodded. "I know that chart. Changing jobs and a death in the family get about the same score, which says something about the average workplace."

I started to reply, but Cleta bustled up with a laden tray. "Here we go. I had one of the rolls earlier. Dorothy outdid herself today." A carafe of coffee and a teapot went on the table first, followed by a flowery cup and saucer in front of me and one of the heavy mugs for Bob. Unmatched dinner plates holding enormous cinnamon rolls, gooey with frosting, settled in front of each of us. "This ought to hold you till lunch."

Bob stared at his roll. He inhaled deeply, closing his eyes at the scent of cinnamon and yeast. "Wow. This ought to hold me till next week."

Cleta chuckled as she bent to lay a plate with an assortment of homemade dog biscuits in front of each dog. "Wait till you see what's on the lunch menu," she told him, straightening. "You'll get hungry again. Okay, doggies, eat up."

Emily Ann and Jack rose, wagging, and started crunching their treats. Cleta smiled down at them before turning to slide the check under the salt shaker. "Everybody all set?"

We nodded, and she headed back into the café. I busied myself pouring tea and adding a little milk to it, then cut a bite of cinnamon roll. It was heaven. I looked across the table at Bob, who was savoring his first bite. "Wow, this is good," he breathed. "Am I ever glad you tried to steal my car this morning."

When Emily Ann and I arrived home later that morning, I flipped open my computer and logged onto the Internet. I typed "Bob Richardson" into the search box on the Google page and sat back to scan the results. More than ten thousand entries were immediately at my disposal. I took off the quotes and added High Cross, but that only increased the number of hits. I tried an advanced search. Ah, now we were down to a mere 2800 or so.

I read the descriptions of several pages. The many obituaries didn't seem appropriate, unless he was a spy or a fugitive who had stolen some dead guy's identity, which struck even my fevered imagination as farfetched. Dozens of genealogy pages beckoned; they might be about this Bob Richardson but I'd never be able to tell. Unfortunately I hadn't thought to ask him his grandmother's maiden name. I saw that I could buy some rather fetching water lilies bred by a Bob Richardson. I noticed as well an artist, a professor, a hypnotist, a floral designer, a minister, a restaurant owner, and a dog groomer, but none of their web pages sported portraits. Too many Bob Richardsons in the world to be able to find a particular one this way.

What I didn't find was any article, about potato

blight or pipeline rivets or anything else, authored by any Bob Richardson.

9

Jack followed me out of Bob's bedroom and down the hall. "Call me old fashioned," I remarked to the dog, "but I would keep my computer on the desk. But I suppose the point of a laptop is you can move it anywhere."

Jack's expression was agreeable. When we reached the living room the dog went to the front window and lifted the sheers with his head to peer out. I inspected the room for a laptop, but saw nothing on the few pieces of furniture or lurking in a corner. The dining room was the same. I walked to the kitchen, which looked as it had last night: clean and quiet. A single coffee mug sat upside down on the counter, and a teaspoon reposed in the sink. I hadn't noticed them last night but I'd been focused on the phone. I turned in a slow circle, then began opening cabinet doors, which proved to hide only the normal kitchen accoutrements of dishes, pans, and food.

Frowning, I tried another hop to check the top of the refrigerator. "The man doesn't have a computer, or he doesn't keep it in the house. Maybe he goes to the public library to use one," I commented. I looked around and realized neither dog had followed me into the room. I always feel much sillier talking out loud to myself than to a dog. I turned to leave the kitchen, and saw a small object on the table in the corner. Three steps, and I picked it up: a printed book of matches. Opened, the outside looked like a business card for a bar called The Last Resort. Small black print on white showed an address and phone number and "G. Harburn, Prop." in the lower right-hand corner.

I turned it over. Inside the name Trixie and a phone number were written in purple ink, the i's dotted with a star and a heart. I frowned. Who was Trixie—could she be the woman in red? I had difficulty imagining that name with the classy suit, but parents are apt to stick any old name on their infants. I myself knew lawyers named Brandy, Junior, and Chip.

By now slanting morning sunlight streamed through the kitchen window. I shoved the matches in my jeans pocket and went the stove to switch off the light over it. As I brought my hand back down, both dogs burst through the kitchen door. Emily Ann, who is usually content to stay on a sofa—any sofa—until it is time to eat or run to, say, Philadelphia, glued herself to my leg. Jack stood with his back to me, facing the front of the house, and growled. A deep, menacing, real growl.

I'd always heard the phrase 'my blood ran cold,' but I hadn't known until then it was actually possible. Both dogs became absolutely still. Jack's hackles were raised. I felt the hairs on the back of my own neck stand up which, combined with my blood running cold, was amazingly uncomfortable—like an ice pack in need of a shave.

I swallowed the big lump of fear in my throat and whispered, "What's the matter?" I edged around the dogs, forcing my stiff legs to carry me across the kitchen to the door. I squinted around the door frame. Through the big window in the living room, where the sheer curtains gave a misty unreality to the view, I could see my car being searched by a strange man. His head was under the open back hatch and he was rummaging in the spare tire compartment. A few feet behind him stood another car, large and black.

Apparently finding nothing, he backed up, and I saw that he was dark-haired and tall, wearing a navy sport coat and khaki slacks that seemed rather formal for searching my car. He walked around to the passenger side, opened the door, and started groping under the seat. I knew nothing was there, and soon he knew it too. He straightened, and turned to look at the house. As he did, sunlight glittered on something metallic at his waist. I'd never seen a gun tucked into a waistband outside a movie, but I was instantly convinced that this was the real thing.

I ducked behind the doorframe. Jack growled again. I looked at him and saw that he was trembling, his tail tucked in tight. His big ears were clamped against his skull, and his lips pulled up to expose the tips of his shining teeth. I risked another peek around the door jamb. The man was walking toward the house.

The next thing I knew I was by the back door, a dog on each side of me. I had no memory of moving—I might have levitated across the room. The door was locked. I didn't see a deadbolt latch to open. It was the old fashioned kind that needs a key to unlock it. Bob must keep a key somewhere close. Hadn't seen one when I searched the kitchen. But one of the keys on his ring must open it. I struggled to get into my pocket for Bob's keys. No, that pocket had the book of matches. The other pocket.

The keys clattered in my shaking hand as I tried one after another. The front door rattled. Had I locked it behind me? I heard the rattle again. The next key I tried slid into the lock. The back door opened. Two tiptoeing leaps and I was across the porch and down the stairs. I grabbed for Emily Ann's leash, and Jack streaked ahead of us into the woods. We ran.

10

I hate to run. I'm not built for it—my legs aren't long enough to work gracefully at more than a fast walk, I have hip joints that creak, and ankles that are perilously prone to turning. I immediately break into a sweat when I move fast, and I hate being hot.

I also hate the woods. Things reach out and grab you or poke you. Poison ivy lurks, and you don't see until you've sat in it or your dog has nosed through it and given you a big kiss on the ear. You can't see where you're going, and you plunge into hidden creeks and trip over leaf-covered logs.

Now I discovered that with sufficient motivation—like a strange man with a gun trying to break in—none of this mattered in the slightest. Jack bounded ahead and I puffed along as fast as I could. Emily Ann, damn her, was barely trotting. Why in the world had I chosen a greyhound? And how come Jack's short legs carried him so much faster than mine?

This particular patch of woods was no better than any other I had been in. Oh, I've read the Gothic novels where the heroine—usually clad in a Victorian high-necked yet diaphanous nightdress and flimsy slippers—is able to narrate a description of every plant as she flees from the villain. "I darted past a towering columbo oak, its pinnate leaves trembling in the wash of moonlight. A nearly impenetrable understory of myanumma bushes, species *Crotoniguestula fogma* if I am not mistaken, writhed their sinuous, twisted branches covered in the tell-tale glaucous leaves of leathery pea green, serrate edges dew bedecked and dripping..."

I am not horticulturally adept, even when no one is chasing me with a gun. I crashed into brambles that I thought were blackberries because of the withered fruit that smeared on my shirt. My socks and jeans got plastered with stick-tights. My right foot squished down on a pallid mushroom and I slipped, wrenching my back as I struggled to stay on my feet. My glasses steamed up. I became aware of a low, growly muttering and realized I was cursing steadily.

I had no idea how far we'd run when I had to stop, get my breath, and wipe off my glasses.

Jack circled back to where Emily Ann and I stood panting. Well, I was panting, Emily Ann was her usual cool, unruffled self; she sat down quietly at my side. I finished drying my lenses and put them back on to survey our surroundings. Behind me, broken twigs and fallen leaves gave evidence of our passage through the underbrush. Bob's house was out of sight, but I didn't know how far away it was. Starting off our dash with a goodly amount of fear-induced adrenalin meant that I had run farther than I'd normally be able to manage. But I hadn't been gliding through the woods like something out of James Fennimore Cooper. It wouldn't be difficult to follow our trail.

I peered through the trees. Off to my left a building stood where the land dipped. Of course we couldn't just walk to it. Oh, no. We had to negotiate a barbed wire fence first. Jack walked under the lowest wire and stood wagging at us from the other side.

The fence posts tilted a little so that the wire sagged encouragingly. I shoved at a couple of the posts, but their off-plumb angle was deceptive—they were still firmly embedded in the rocky ground. I pushed down the top strand of wire, but it was too far off the ground for me to swing my leg over without endangering portions of my anatomy that were extremely reluctant to encounter barbed wire.

I looped Emily Ann's leash over one of the posts and pushed down on the second strand of wire and up on the top strand. My right foot went through to the ground on the other side. I had to let go of the top strand to bend over and slide my body through, and my shirt caught on a barb and ripped. I cursed as I wobbled, balancing on the right foot as I brought the left past the barbs. I thought I was all the way through when I realized that my hair, short as it was, had tangled with a barb. The time it took to free it gave me a chance to think about when I had last had a tetanus shot. When I was finally through, I held up the bottom strand as far as I could and coaxed Emily Ann through. She might have been able to leap over the top, but I couldn't take a chance on her getting ensnared by the wire.

Throughout my negotiations with the fence, my heart pounded as hard as when I had been running. My imagination created vivid scenes in which I heard a shot a split second before being pierced by a bullet. The short tragic film ended with the villain burying me in these woods and never being caught, while Kay spent the rest of her life wondering where I was.

The building I'd seen proved to be an old barn, not very large, built into the side of the hill so that you could enter either floor from ground level. The foundation, made of the same stone as Bob's house, supported boards weathered to silver.

I took a deep breath and listened. Birds still sang their morning chorus, in the distance traffic hummed, and Jack shuffled through fallen leaves as he sniffed at the base of the upper-level door. Both dogs were calm, so I went over and pulled at the door. The hinges gave a loud creak but the door opened easily.

Inside, slanted morning light streamed through two windows high in the wall as well as gaps between the boards. A drift of leaves and a few stray pieces of paper—some faded gum wrappers, an old flyer for someone's gardening business—decorated the floor. Jack went to a stack of hay bales piled near one wall and gave them a searching examination with his nose. They looked old; dull and faded and not fragrant like I think of hay being. Jack gave a huge sneeze; they must be full of dust.

A sudden rustling in one corner riveted both dogs' attention, and Jack hopped over to check out the source of the noise. He sniffed and snuffled, while I held my breath, fervently hoping that no mice—or worse—would come running across the boards toward me. Whatever it was remained hidden, and Jack gave up the search to follow his nose across the floor to the wall.

A narrow, steep staircase went down into the gloom below. Jack walked his front feet down a couple of steps, stopped, and looked back at me. "We'll explore another time," I told him. "Right now it's dark down there and I don't have a flashlight and that guy is following us. You're the one who wanted to run away from him, remember? We need to get going."

Emily Ann sneezed delicately from the position she'd taken beside me.

"Come on, let's figure out how to get out of these woods," I said.

Jack came back to stand by me. I turned toward the door. Jack pricked his ears and growled. He was looking toward the stairway that led into the lower part of the building. Before I could react, hinges creaked and more light flooded in as the lower door was opened.

Except for the intake of breath that caught in my throat, I was frozen in place. The dogs became statues. Jack gave the faintest of growls, but the pounding of my heart was as likely to be heard.

The door downstairs creaked again. I imagined the man in the sport coat and slacks holding the door and looking around. A heavy gun gleamed in his hand. Just when I thought I would scream with fear and frustration, the elderly hinges spoke once more. The light dimmed. Silence from below. He must have gone back outside.

I wanted nothing more than to dash out the door we'd come in, but we would run right into him. I looked around hastily. I could climb down the ladder and hide in the space he'd already seen, but I couldn't leave the dogs. I flung myself behind the bales of hay that Jack had inspected earlier. Wedged my back between the bales and the wall and drew up my knees. Emily Ann pressed against my side. Jack scrambled between my knees and my chest. We'd barely squeezed into place when the door into the upper level creaked. I felt as much as heard the heavy footsteps on the wooden floorboards.

The footsteps came closer and my nose began to tickle.

It must be a nearly uncontrollable human compulsion to sneeze when you're hiding. I've always been skeptical when someone in a book or movie just has to sneeze at the worst possible time. Now I realized it was a cliché based on true human experience. Of course, surrounding oneself with dusty hay might be a contributing factor.

I held my breath. I could hear his breathing across the few feet that separated us. I caught the mingled scent of aftershave and cigarette smoke. I wiggled my nose to distract it. Didn't help. My right arm was around Emily Ann's shoulders. I moved just enough to pinch my nostrils shut. That slight movement made the floorboard creak.

Absolute silence. Then one more heavy tread thudded on the old floorboards. What should I say when he found me? I hoped I could come up with something wittier than "Dr. Livingston, I presume?" Or would he just shoot me before I had time to say anything? Then on the other side of the hay bales little paws scrabbled and a tiny voice squeaked.

From a point far too close to our hiding place, the intruder sucked in his breath and jumped back, hitting the old floorboards with a resounding thud. I clenched my eyes shut, praying for him to go crashing through to the floor below. No such luck. He said loudly, "Shit! Stupid mouse." Jack and Emily Ann and I held our breath.

And then a dog barked outside, not far away. To my ears it didn't sound like either Jack or Emily Ann, but it diverted our follower. His footsteps hastened toward the door. Hinges creaked, and again as the door banged shut. Silence held the barn.

Gradually the pounding of my heart slowed and my breathing became that of a person sitting down instead of a marathon runner or a fleeing Victorian heroine. The sneeze must have been scared right out of me, for now my nose was fine. A new discomfort edged into my awareness—the hay bales were making me itch. A sweatshirt and jeans were scant protection from their prickliness.

It took a while to let go of the dogs. I finally loosed my arms from around Jack and Emily Ann and whispered, "Okay, guys, I think we can get up now."

They both shook themselves hard when they got outside the confines of the bales; the whipping sound of Jack's long ears seemed thunderous. I froze again, but the man did not reappear. My knees had locked and I had to crawl out of my cocoon and lean on a bale to hoist myself back to my feet. I dusted pieces of hay off my clothing and scratched the itches that I could reach. Finally we crept to the door.

I pushed it open a couple of inches to peek outside and listen. Other than the normal—what I assumed were normal—bird and breeze noises the morning was quiet, and neither dog seemed to hear anything untoward. I trusted their hearing far more than my own. We slipped outside.

A path beaten in the withered grass encircled the barn. I turned to the left and tramped down the hill that the structure was built into. Reaching the front corner, I took a cautious peek and saw that an old road ran past double doors in the center of the barn's lower level and continued in the direction of Bob's house. It was patchy with grass and weeds and couldn't have had a tractor using it for years. Walking the road would be easier and faster than continuing haphazardly through the woods. Also, given my level of navigational skills, if I followed a road I was more likely to actually arrive somewhere.

I could only hope that the man who'd followed us had gone back toward Bob's house. I decided if I saw him I would duck into the woods and either get away or make myself look like a tree.

11

Emily Ann, Jack and I walked a few hundred yards, around a bend and out of sight of the barn. It started to rain. I paused to look at the sky. While we had been running through the woods, the sun had disappeared behind a wall of gray. Now the clouds had reached critical mass and a cold downpour drummed on our heads.

I started along the rough road again, hurrying but no longer running. Jack lifted his face appreciatively to the sky as he took a long sniff. Emily Ann shook herself. I growled.

The pause in the barn had let me catch my breath, but in no other way was I any happier. My face was chilled but I was uncomfortably hot inside my jeans and sweatshirt, and I itched in various places, including several that could not be addressed in public. Hay had worked its way inside my shirt and fallen partway down my back. The weight of my fanny pack

76

increased half a pound with every step. My glasses were steamed up on the inside and rain spotted on the outside. I took them off and wiped them but my wet sweatshirt only made a smeary blur.

With my glasses back on, I saw that the trees ahead were thinning. We hurried forward, and I saw houses, ranch houses built in the Sixties, huddled on their grassy plots. We had come out of the woods and reached suburbia.

The old farm road petered out between two chain-link-fenced yards, ending at a curving street. The day was still early, perhaps 9:00 or a little later. Children would be in school and their parents gone to work. If anyone was around they were safe and dry inside. The street had the deserted air of a town in a science fiction film where everyone has been spirited away.

Even with no traffic, I didn't want to leave Jack leashless on the street. He's a bright guy but any dog can get distracted by a cat or squirrel at just the wrong moment. I took Emily Ann's leash and threaded it through his collar and looped it around once. I had no idea of which way to turn. I could see intersections in both directions. "What do you guys think?" I asked. Emily Ann unhesitatingly turned right, and Jack and I followed her.

And followed her and followed her. Who decided back in the Fifties or Sixties that neighborhoods should consist of winding streets? Each led into another and curved around. I could hear traffic noises indicating signs of life somewhere off in the distance, but I couldn't get there. Every street looked like the one we had just walked down. We walked and walked, getting wetter and wetter. I became convinced that we must be going in circles and tried to pay attention to the houses at each corner, but their identifying details ran together in my brain until every house looked alike.

A couple of times a car hurried past on its way to the outside world or to home and warmth and comfort. I thought about flagging one down to ask how to get out of this place, which set off an argument in my head about the wisdom of doing so. The shy voice said it was too embarrassing to be lost in a residential neighborhood. The alarmist added that anyone I stopped would think I was insane and probably call the cops, and with my luck it would be Chief Johnson who came to arrest me. The practical one said we're bound to find our way out eventually, and to keep moving.

Whenever I paused to look around, the dogs would shake their accumulated rain onto me. I wished I could do the same; my wet clothes sagged more with each step. Thank heavens I'd worn jeans; pants with an elastic waist could have spelled disaster.

At last I saw a neon glow against the cloud-darkened sky, and was able to keep making turns toward it. We reached the entrance to the tract and I recognized where I was—about a mile and a half from Bob's driveway. I turned right and stumped up a straight stretch that in a car would seem flat, but actually had a steady rise. I felt as though I'd been tramping around for years.

The neon glow grew brighter, and at last I reached a Texaco station with two covered bays for gas pumps and the usual little attendant's booth with a cash register behind a counter and a rack of tired looking snacks. And—wonder of wonders—a pay phone at the edge of the lot.

I hauled out my wallet from the fanny pack. It held a five and six ones, and seventeen cents in change.

I walked to the counter and laid a dollar down in front of the attendant, a vacant-eyed man wearing a shirt that looked suspiciously like a pajama top. "Could I get some change for the phone please?" I asked.

He managed to focus on me, and then on the dollar bill. He shook his head. "Uh uh, I can't just give out money. You gotta buy something."

I found it necessary to close my eyes and breathe deeply so I would not scream at him. When I opened them again, Jack was looking worriedly up at me. Suppressing a wish that my companions looked more threatening, I glanced around to see what I could buy. Mints and gum and little cellophane bags of salted nuts and odd brands of candy bars I didn't recognize hung limply from the rack. Everything looked faded and old, and even though I was beyond hungry I saw nothing in this place I could bear to put into my mouth. I finally picked up a package of chewing gum that claimed to have eight sticks of mouth poppin' cinnamint flavor and laid it on the counter next to the dollar.

Pajama Man rang up eighty-nine cents on his cash register. The drawer popped open and he fished for a dime and a penny.

"Wait a minute," I said quickly, realizing he was about to close the drawer again. I could be buying stale candy all day. "I need change for the phone. Give me some quarters while you have the drawer open." I pulled another dollar out of my billfold.

He frowned and looked at the two bills. "Um..."

I was really going to have to teach these dogs to bite people. I'd think about how later. Now I was seized with inspiration. I picked the two dollar bills up and put them back in my billfold, and handed him the five. Instantly his brow cleared. "Uh, okay," he said.

"And be sure to give me four quarters for one of the dollars," I reminded him. He managed to oblige. I heaved a sigh of relief and turned away from the counter with my change.

"Um, ma'am, you forgot your gum," he called after me.

I turned and he was holding it out, smiling. "You know what?" I said. "I just needed the change. You can have the gum."

His smile got bigger, and I realized how young he was. "Gosh, thanks," he said.

I waved to him and decided to postpone biting lessons for the dogs. "Come on, pups," I muttered. "Let's call someone to give us a ride."

They trotted obediently at my side. As we emerged from under the high canopy over the pumps, the rain renewed our general wetness. The phone's

80

height was awkward, the top of its stainless steel hood reaching my chin. What had happened to phone booths you could step into and sit down, those quaint, old fashioned ones with a door you could close? No doubt they had been supplanted by cell phones and the driver's seat of a car.

I leaned against the too-short booth, realizing with a pang that Bob would be my first choice of someone to call for a ride. That obviously wasn't an option.

I should call Kay and have her fetch me. But I didn't know what time the furniture was being picked up—Kay had said dawn which could mean anything from five a.m. to ten or so. She would need to be at the store.

I could call the police; after all, I'd been chased by a man with a gun. At least I thought he had a gun. Chief Johnson couldn't still be on duty, could he? Surely he didn't work around the clock. I considered whether explaining the whole thing to someone new would be worse that talking to Chief Johnson again. But he would have told the next person on duty about the events he had handled on his shift.

The sarcastic inner voice piped up. "Can't you just hear him? 'It was a busy night. I did a routine traffic stop and it was Kay Chelton's crazy cousin claiming her boyfriend had been kidnapped by a space alien posing as a blonde in a red suit. Later she called to tell me about a message the space aliens had beamed down onto the boyfriend's phone machine.'"

"Stop it, it was Kay who added the space alien

bit," I said out loud. The dogs pricked their ears at me. I reached for the phone. "I'll just tell the police we were chased by a man with a gun."

The police officer in my head asked, "And what kind of gun was it, Mrs. McGuire? Oh, you didn't get close enough to see? You say it was tucked into his waistband and you saw it through a set of white organdy sheers?"

I couldn't do it. I ran through a mental list of other people I'd gotten to know in the few months I'd been back in Willow Falls. They were acquaintances, people you said hello to when you passed them in the street. I had met several friendly people at the dog park, but I didn't know anyone's last name. A tattered phone book was tucked under the phone, but the phone book is not enlightened enough to list people by their dogs' names.

I pulled out the book, looked up a number. Dialed for a cab.

The ladies' room beckoned next; I didn't want to look so scary the cab driver would refuse to pick me up. Both dogs shook themselves hard as soon as I closed the door behind us. Luckily they were just wet, not muddy, so a few paper towels erased the evidence of their ablutions from the walls and floor. They panted happily at me, shiny and eager for whatever would come next.

I, on the other hand, felt like a refugee from a junkyard. Only so much damage to one's appearance can be repaired with cold water and paper towels in a Texaco restroom. In my case it made no appreciable difference. Twigs of hay stuck out of the hair plastered to my skull. Mud streaked up my cheek, partially covering a scratch on my forehead. My wet clothes clung to me in a clammy embrace. My face was flushed and my neck blotchy and overheated. Mushroom goo smeared one knee, and a liberal coating of stick-tights decorated my jeans from the hems on up. My shoes squished as I shifted my weight. I was probably lucky the cashier had waited on me at all.

"Blagh," I scowled at my reflection. I don't waste space in my fanny pack on cosmetics or cleaning equipment. A few wet paper towels took care of the mud, and I fluffed as much water as I could out of my hair with my fingers. I made a face at myself in the mirror, and left the restroom to wait for the cab.

It took forever to arrive. After a few minutes I sat down on the curb by the attendant's booth. When the taxi finally pulled into the drive I hauled myself to my feet. The white station wagon, several years old, was emblazoned with the name of the cab company and its phone number painted in purple and red on the doors. I pulled open the back passenger door. Emily Ann stepped in and lay down by the far door as Jack bounced in.

"Hey, lady," the cabbie protested as I slid my wet butt onto the seat, "I don't take no dogs in here." He peered at me over thick glasses perched halfway down his long nose. A stout man in his early sixties, he sported the kind of stubble on his face that always looks like a three day growth of beard, no matter when it was last shaved off. Jack put his short front legs on the back of the front seat and laid his muzzle on them, giving the driver a soulful look. His tail wagged madly. "What the hell," the driver shrugged. "Where you goin'?"

"Two twenty three Maple," I told him and settled back for the ride.

12

Two Weeks Earlier

Cleta came out of the café with a carafe of boiling water to refresh my tea. "Kay called," she told me. "She wants you to come by when you finish your breakfast."

Trellis Island's Eileen had finished her coffee and hightailed it to my cousin's store. "Sure," I said to Cleta. "Thanks for the message."

"Kay is your cousin?" Bob asked, surprise coloring his voice. "How did she know where to find you?"

"Kay has her little ways," I said.

"Do the two of you have a deep psychic connection or something?"

"No, thank heavens! You just don't know how small Willow Falls is yet."

He took a sip of coffee. "You said you inherited your parents' house. Is that where you grew up?" he asked. I shook my head.

"No, my parents bought this one after I'd left

85

for college." When I had gone home for Christmas my freshman year I'd found that from now on I would stay in my parents' guest room, that I no longer had a room in their house. They had seen nothing odd in the arrangement. "I haven't decided yet if I want to keep it or buy something else."

He nodded. "You probably keep seeing your parents in it."

I nodded.

"Which might be a comfort depending on how you felt about them," he continued.

Whether he was a reporter or not, it was too soon to have that conversation. I took a bite of my roll to buy some time. After I swallowed I said, "What about you? What brought you to Willow Falls?"

He shrugged. "I've been living in High Cross, and I got a chance to rent a place here for less money. I can write anywhere, but I recently got Jack and the new place has room for him to run around more than he could in the city." He looked down at his pet, now sprawled on his side, panting gently.

"Is he a pound puppy?" I asked.

Bob shook his head. "I guess you could call him a rescue dog. I ended up with him when his former owner died."

"Do you have a map of Willow Falls? I could mark the location of the dog park," I offered. "Or if you want, I could take you sometime." I tried to sound offhand.

"That would be great. Jack loves to play with other dogs." Bob sipped some more coffee. I couldn't

86

tell if he wanted my company or a map, and I wasn't sure how to ask. I'd used up all my brazenness with 'are you married.'

Bob's focus shifted to something beyond me. I glanced over my shoulder. Two women were crossing Maple, and a large black car paused before turning left onto Second Street. I turned back around. Bob was staring at the street, his fingers around the coffee mug white with the force of his grip. A more delicate cup would have been in shards.

"Are you okay?" I asked.

He pulled his gaze back to me. "What? Yes. I—I thought I saw a car I knew." He set the mug carefully on the table. "Not very likely though."

"Somebody you knew in High Cross? Maybe they'll circle the block and you can catch them."

"Let's hope not. Come to think of it, this guy might be perfect for Doris."

"Ahh," I nodded. "Not a friend."

"Definitely not."

I ate the last bite of my roll and put down the fork. "Well, thanks for breakfast," I said.

"Could I tag along to your cousin's store?" he asked. "I'd enjoy seeing it. Maybe I'll find something I've always been looking for. Oh, but I've got Jack."

"That's okay, she'll love him. She's between dogs herself right now but Emily Ann hangs around whenever I'm there. We use her as a prop to highlight whatever sofas Kay has in stock. Emily Ann is a total couch potato, unless she's outdoors running. But if Doris is there the one running will be me." I had a happy thought. "Unless you think we could get Jack to bite her."

He grinned. "It's not natural to him, but he's very trainable. Perhaps Emily Ann could show him how."

"Nah, she prefers a withering sneer. She stands up as tall as she can and stares down her nose at you."

As we left the patio, Bob looked both ways along Maple Street, swinging his little pack over his left shoulder. If Doris was still around, she was safely inside one of the shops. We walked the half block to OKay Antiques, where Bob paused to study the display in the window. Kay and I had set up a cozy library corner, with worn leather-bound volumes in a glass-fronted barrister's bookcase next to a plump little settee. A small, round oak table was near, its top covered with an embroidered cloth. A pair of wire-framed glasses rested on an old-fashioned novel by a green-shaded lamp. In front of the settee was a small Turkish carpet, with a pair of needlepoint slippers apparently kicked off and abandoned.

"Nice," he commented, holding the door open for me.

I unclipped Emily Ann's leash as we crossed the threshold. She started to climb into the display to curl up on the settee, but I said, "Emily Ann, go to Kay! You have to say hello before you lie down." Obediently she walked over to Kay, gave her a nuzzle, then with her nose in the air and a sideways look at me went back and made herself part of the display.

Kay was at the sales counter wrapping a package to ship. She laid down the dispenser of heavy tape and grinned at us. She flicked me a sideways glance in a way I knew well. "Hey, Louisa."

"Cleta said you wanted me. Kay, this is Bob and Jack. They're new in town."

Kay held her hand out over the counter. "Hi, Bob. Louisa's got you off to a good start if she took you to the Bluebird."

"That's for sure. I will dream of that cinnamon roll. It's nice to meet you," Bob said, smiling at my cousin and shaking hands.

She turned to me. "You will never guess who was just in here."

"Doris Carter," Bob and I said in chorus. Kay gawped at us. "We met her on the street," I went on, "and Bob told her this was a good place to shop because he could see it over her shoulder and he thought it might get rid of her. Did she buy anything? Her money would have cooties on it."

"I never take money with cooties," Kay said.

"Did she recognize you?" I asked. "I figured you'd remember her."

"Of course I remember her. I still want to punch her for that trailer trash remark she made at the funeral," Kay snorted.

Bob's eyebrows rose. "Trailer trash?"

I made a quick motion to stop her from saying more. It didn't work.

"Doris is one of those people who thinks anyone from the Midwest grew up poor and barefoot," she said. "She stood in the middle of Louisa's living room

89

after Roger had just been buried—"

"Kay," I said.

"—and had everyone laughing about the 'trailer trash way to redecorate' because Louisa had thrown out a bunch of Roger's things. Well, first she threw Roger out—"

"Kay!"

"—after which she dumped everything he owned on the front lawn, where it all got rained on, which you could pretty much count on in Seattle. After years of putting up with him, Louisa finally turned into something off an afternoon talk show and started chucking silk underwear and titanium tennis rackets and—"

"Kay! Bob is not interested in this," I said from between clenched teeth. I wished I had one of the specially-ordered tennis balls that had gone with the titanium tennis racket, to stuff into Kay's mouth.

"—and she threw his computer out an upstairs window, and probably six hundred CDs, and—"

I raised my voice. "At least Doris isn't here now." And at least she didn't say all this embarrassing stuff to Bob, who looked amused. "Did she speak to you?"

Kay switched gears effortlessly. "She barely registered my presence. For a lawyer she's not very observant. She strolled in, looked at a couple of things, and asked me if we ship large pieces. I said no and she left."

"But we ship large pieces all the time," I protested.

"Not to her. Her money has cooties on it, remember?" She looked down and noticed Jack. "Say, you are a cutie pie. What was your name? Jack? Those are impressive ears. If they went up instead of down you could be a Jack rabbit instead of a Jack dog."

His tail whirled at his name and the short front legs pranced a little. He looked ready to do some bunny hopping if that was what was called for.

"Mind if I look around?" Bob asked. He gestured toward a looming hulk of oak across the room and walked toward it. "I can't figure out what this piece of furniture is supposed to be."

Kay shook her head ruefully, following him. "Ah, yes, my Albatross. Isn't it hideous?" The piece in question stood by the wide arch that led into a larger showroom, stuffed with furniture and an incredible variety of objects that someone might someday want. The Albatross was a monstrosity of quarter sawn oak. "I must have been out of my mind the day I bought it. I was at an auction and I'd bought a couple of really good pieces for fabulous prices. I guess it went to my head."

She ran her hand over the oak surface as she walked around the piece. "It's a combination of a sideboard and desk, with room for wine bottles and a place to hang a few clothes. I think it was custom made for a rich eccentric who lived in one room or something. All it lacks is a bed that lets down out of one side. I thought it was funny at the time but I am never going to sell the darned thing. You'll probably have to bury me in it because I can't see it leaving the store any other way. You'll need to line up more than six pall-bearers though, it weighs a ton and a half. Oh well, everyone's entitled to a few mistakes, right?" She gave the Albatross a friendly pat. Turning to me she said, "Say, Louisa, I need you to run an errand for me. Bob, could you excuse us for two seconds?"

He nodded and said, "Sure." He turned to the Albatross and began opening drawers.

Kay grabbed my wrist and towed me back to her office under the stairway that leads up to her apartment. Closing the door, she hissed, "Louisa, where in the world did you pick him up? Edward the mailman was here saying you were at the Bluebird with a man who has a golden aura, and Eileen from Trellis Island came in and said she'd seen you with Jeremy Irons. Except she thinks he has a better butt than Jeremy Irons."

"I didn't pick him up. I wouldn't know how. I came out of the lawyer's office and our cars are identical and I was trying to put my key in his lock—"

"Well, as long as it wasn't the other way around," she sniggered. "After all, you did just meet."

I ignored the interruption. "—and he thought I was trying to steal his car. Then the dogs met each other and we started talking and he hasn't met anybody here yet so we went to the Bluebird. That's it."

"That's it, huh? You seemed very chummy when you walked in here."

"Grow up. We're not in high school any more. He's a nice person but I've only known him about an hour."

She reached over and gave me a hug. "Well, an hour is a good start. I like him. Your taste in men is improving."

"But Kay, he told me he's a freelance writer. What if he really picked *me* up because he's writing something about Roger?"

She blinked. "Why would anyone want to do that?"

"Because Roger died in the stupidest circumstances and got himself plastered all over the papers. Maybe he's doing an article on lawyers who die undignified deaths. I don't know."

"Louisa, no one cares about how Roger died," she assured me. "It's been six months. Old news is dead news."

I bit my lower lip, wanting to believe her. "Do you really have an errand for me?"

"Of course not, that was just to get you alone."

"What's he going to think when I come back empty handed?"

"Stop worrying about what everybody thinks. He'll think I gave you a very small errand. Or that we were talking about him. Here." She picked two pieces of a broken plate out of the wastebasket and thrust them into my hands. "You can say you're taking this to be repaired."

"Do you want me to take it for repair?" It was a nothing plate as far as I could see.

"No, take it home and throw it away. And throw away some of your worries at the same time."

13

The taxi's meter read $17.40 when we reached Kay's shop. I told the driver to wait while I stepped inside for some money. The dogs followed me onto the streaming pavement, and the steady drizzle re-plastered my hair to skull.

Inside, Kay and a broad-shouldered man were gazing down at a blueprint spread on the sales counter. As the door opened he was saying, "—going to take all my tricks to make a space that seats over three hundred feel like a cozy English tea room. These may well be the most tasteless people who have ever bespoken my services." At the jangle of the bell over the door, he looked over his shoulder. It was Kay's friend Ambrose. His lips twitched as he took in my bedraggled appearance. "Ah, Louisa, how delightful to see you."

"Um, hi. Kay, I need—" Emily Ann surged forward to greet Ambrose, pulling me and Jack with her.

"Emily Ann, wait," I said, leaning over to snap the leash from her collar and unwind it from Jack's. Both dogs rushed to Ambrose, and Emily Ann leaned on him adoringly. Fortunately her ultra short hair didn't hold much water and his natty clothing—today a taupe silk turtleneck and brown slacks topped with a brown tweed vest shot through with threads in amethyst, navy and emerald—was none the worse for her attentions.

Ambrose patted her enthusiastically before turning to Jack. "Well hello, you handsome boy," he said. Jack accepted a pat on the head, then danced and bucked his way to Kay. She stooped to pick up his long ears and held them straight up. "Jack, sweetie!" she crooned. "Is he just an old bunny? Who's the rabbit? Who's got the bunny ears?"

"Kay, I need some—"

She dropped Jack's ears, gave his butt a pat, and straightened to look at me. "Jeez, Lou, what the hell have you been doing?" Her eyebrows shot up. "You look like you've been on one of those awful TV reality shows. And lost."

"I need seventeen dollars to pay for the cab," I said.

"Cab? What cab? Where's your car?"

Ambrose headed for the door. "I've got it," he said. I started to protest. "No, no, my treat, dear Louisa," he said. Through the window we saw him pull money from his pocket and hand it in to the cab driver. He straightened and gave a little wave, and hurried back inside.

"I'll be on my way for now," he said to Kay. "Could you lunch on Thursday to talk more about my little project?"

She nodded. "Latish would be good for me, say one thirty. Meet at the Bluebird?"

"Wonderful. That sounds perfect. Louisa, I hope to see you again soon," and he was out the door once more. He paused while closing the door, stuck his head back in and said, "Kay, thanks for letting the guys pick up that piece so early this morning."

"You bet," she said. When he was gone she turned to me. "Louisa, are you okay? You look like a drowned rat. Where is your car? Is this part of the Bob thing?"

"I'm all right, I'm just wet."

"What happened?"

"I went to Bob's house to see if he was back, and I looked out and saw a guy searching my car. The dogs and I ran away through the woods and we found an old barn and the guy followed us and we had to hide behind some hay bales. Then we got lost in suburbia and when I finally found a phone I called a cab and came here. What time is it, anyway?"

Her mouth opened and closed a couple of times but for once Kay was at a loss for words. "Almost eleven," she said at last.

"No wonder I'm so hungry." I gave an involuntary shiver. My clothes had reached a perfection of clamminess, and my shoes made little slurping noises with every move. "All I had before I left home was some juice."

"You're soaked through," she fussed, reaching over to feel the sleeve of my soggy sweatshirt. "Go upstairs, take a shower and put on something dry. After that you can tell me what happened. Go on, I'll take care of the dogs."

I obeyed, my climb up the steps to her apartment slowed by the heavy tiredness that comes after an overload of adrenalin. I went to the tiny back bedroom where I sometimes spend the night. I'd left a few clothes in the closet, and it was utter luxury to be able to grab dry jeans, a soft old cotton sweater, clean socks and underwear to change into. I stayed in the shower long enough for the hot water to loosen my neck muscles, cranking up the heat every few minutes. When I emerged Kay was at the kitchen counter constructing sandwiches, the two dogs nearby, waiting for any scraps that might fall.

My stomach gave a lurch at the sight of the food. I hurried across the room. "You may have just saved my life," I breathed, grabbing one and talking through a big bite. I tasted Swiss cheese and toasted walnuts and a little tomato chutney.

"Well, that was easy." She frowned at me. "Now swallow that, and tell me what is going on."

I held up one finger as I bit off more. Chewing, I reached into a nearby cabinet for a glass, which I filled with milk. I'd never have a better day for comfort food. I took a swig, then set the glass back down. "Like I said, I went to Bob's to see if he'd come back. I spent a few minutes checking out the house, and when I was in the kitchen Jack ran in looking scared. I looked out front and a guy was searching my car."

"Why didn't you call the cops?" she demanded.

I hate sentences that start out with "why didn't you." You're on the defensive before you even open your mouth. "It looked like he had a gun—"

"A gun! Are you sure?"

"I thought he did. He'd tucked it into his waist-band. He started toward the house, and I didn't have time to do anything but run. We left out the back door and ran into the woods."

She made an exasperated noise I knew well. "That's even more reason to call the police!"

"Kay, a guy with a gun was coming to the door. I was afraid. I didn't think of picking up the phone, I just got the hell out of there."

"Okay, okay, I can see that. Especially after Bob took off last night. Anybody would have been spooked."

"Exactly."

"But even if running into the woods seemed like the right thing to do, you could have called the cops or me for that matter while you were running away. Where the hell was the cell phone I gave you?"

"It's in the glove box of my car," I said sheepish-ly.

She threw up her hands and gave a disgusted snort. "You and your thing about phones. They are useful, modern devices that can save you a great deal of trouble."

"Okay, okay," I tried to placate her.

"All right, sit down. I want to hear everything

in more detail." She put the other sandwich on a plate and picked it up.

"Can't I have another sandwich?" I tried to keep the whine out of my voice. "I didn't have any breakfast. I figured I'd go to Bob's for two seconds and eat afterwards."

"All right, take this one," she said, thrusting the plate into my hands and turning back to make another for herself. I refilled my glass and took that and the plate to the table. My usual chair, to the right of Kay's at the head of the table, had yesterday's High Cross paper in it. I moved the paper to the recycling bin and sat down, taking another big bite. By the time I finished chewing, Kay had joined me with her sandwich, a glass of iced tea, and a crystal water glass filled with carrot sticks. I pulled one out and crunched it.

"What kind of gun was it?" she asked, picking up her tea. She sipped, waiting for my answer.

"I don't know. A gun. It was tucked into his waistband. I've never understood why a guy would do that. Aren't they afraid it will go off and, um, injure them?"

"Wait a minute. You said you were in the kitchen, looking toward the front of the house, and you saw him outside by your car?" I nodded and she went on. "And from that distance you could tell he had a gun in his britches?"

"When he turned toward the house I saw the sun glint off of metal. At his waist." The more I talked the less sure I was that I had ever seen the sun glint off anything in my life. I couldn't remember if I had said anything about the sheers still being across the windows. Nothing would drag that detail out of me now.

"I thought it was raining."

"It started after we ran away. Earlier it was sunny."

"Louisa! It could have been his belt buckle or something! Jeez, I don't believe this. You must have gotten really spooked last night." She shook her head and picked up her sandwich.

"Well, I did," I admitted. "And it's been more than twelve hours and I haven't heard from Bob."

"Have you checked your message machine at home this morning?" she said around a bite of sandwich.

I shook my head. "I haven't been back home, remember? I came straight here."

"Use my phone and call your machine and have it play your messages."

"It can do that?"

She stared at me. "What planet have you been living on? Just call it up and when the machine picks up, punch in your code—" She broke off when she saw my expression. "You have no idea what your code is. Of course."

I ate another carrot stick. Finally I said, "Can you drive me to Bob's so I can get my car back? Or I guess I should call the police from here and tell them about the guy that chased me."

"In a few minutes. First I want you to go over

again what happened last night. You stopped at the Food Right, and he went in and you stayed in the car?" I nodded. "What time was this?"

"I wasn't wearing my watch. We went to the four o'clock movie and had dinner out at the winery, so it was probably eight thirty or a little later."

"How long before he came out?"

"Maybe five minutes. I don't know. I was playing with the radio."

"And he came out with a woman?"

I described again how they had been walking close together and gotten in the same side of the car, and that I had followed as soon as I was able to get into the driver's seat.

"And you're sure it was that Mercedes you followed all the way to the highway?" She took a bite of sandwich and frowned as she chewed.

"I'm sure," I told her, "though I didn't see if they got on the highway or went straight because I was busy with your police chief. Why do you ask?"

She swallowed. "He's not my police chief. And I'm just grasping at straws. It's no wonder Ed couldn't do anything, there's nothing to get hold of. How about when you were at Bob's house this morning? Did you see any clues?"

I shrugged. "How the heck would I know if something is a clue or not?"

"But you searched the house?" I nodded, and she asked, "What did you see?"

"He doesn't own much stuff. Or maybe he didn't move it all here from High Cross. I was sort of looking for his computer, in case he had contacts listed on it, but I didn't find one." I thought about Bob's house. "I didn't go through everything, but I didn't see any pictures, no photos I mean, no letters, no bills even. I looked in his dresser—"

"Any interesting undies?" she asked brightly.

"No," I made a face at her. "Just normal old boxers, although one pair did have pictures of canaries on the fabric. But they looked pretty new so maybe he doesn't wear them." I remembered the ostentatiously expensive silk briefs that my husband had preferred. Boxers with canaries on them seemed incredibly wholesome by comparison.

"How about his checkbook? If we got his old address in High Cross from the checks we might be able to find out something about him."

Her question made me realize something. "You know, I've never seen him pay for anything that wasn't with cash." I thought back over the past two weeks. "I mean, I use my debit card all the time, and before that I always wrote checks. And I use my card to get cash at the ATM."

Kay was nodding. "Hmm, no credit or debit cards used. Could it be a guy thing? How did Roger pay for stuff?"

"He preferred to have someone else pay if he could manage it. Otherwise he used his American Express card."

"One more way Bob is nothing like Roger," she said. "When someone is on the run in books and movies they avoid using cards for fear of being traced that way."

"On the run?" I repeated. "What are you suggesting?"

She shrugged and gave me a quick look. "We don't know a whole lot about Bob," she said. "He could be anyone or anything. He seems to have plenty of free time, and he's a little young to have retired. Maybe he's a writer, and maybe he's not. I think you're wrong about him being a reporter. I couldn't find anything on the Internet in any paper by someone with that name—"

"Kay! You looked him up on the Internet?" I decided not to mention that I had done the same thing.

"Of course. He has an awfully common name. It could be an alias."

"If it is, he could actually be a reporter. Or the prince of a small Balkan country for all we know."

"Right. A prince would be good, you could be Princess Louisa, that has a nice Victorian sound—" She broke off as I made gagging gestures, then went on, "—or maybe he's independently wealthy like you and wants to keep it quiet—"

"Hardly wealthy," I countered. "I just have low expenses. Having no house payment makes a big difference."

"Don't get me wrong, I like Bob, but being kidnapped out of a grocery store is *not* normal behavior, at least not for anyone I've ever known."

This was a telling point; Kay's circle of acquaintances is wide.

"I still think it's odd that I couldn't find a computer," I said. "How can anyone can be a writer these days without one?"

"That is strange. I guess some people still write in longhand but wouldn't a freelance writer need to be online? Have you seen him with a laptop? How about in his car?" I shook my head, and she continued. "The prince theory is looking better. Could a laptop be what the guy was looking for in your car? Maybe Bob has files on one that he's blackmailing someone with—"

I sat up straighter in my chair. "Bob is not blackmailing anyone," I said, scowling at my cousin. "Maybe that man was a panhandler looking for loose change. Maybe—"

"Okay, okay, keep your shirt on," she said. "I don't think Bob's a blackmailer. I'm just speculating. We know next to nothing about him, and only what he himself has told us."

We ate in silence.

"How about the guy searching your car?" she finally asked.

"What about him?"

"What did he look like? Could he have been Bob?"

"No. Why would Bob search my car? Plus, this guy had a completely different body type, and anyway, Jack was really growling. He'd never growl at Bob. This guy was as tall as Bob but way wider."

"Wider like fat?"

I shook my head. "No. Broad shoulders and long arms. He had on a sport coat and khakis, but you could put him in a gorilla suit and he'd be completely convincing."

"And he really followed you?"

"Yes. I'm sure it was him. We found this old barn built into a hillside, and I was on the upper level when I heard someone downstairs. So we hid, and then the door opened upstairs just a few feet from where we were."

"Good lord," Kay breathed, patting her chest.

"Jack knew it was the same person. I've never heard him growl before. I was scared," I admitted.

"Sheesh, I'm getting scared too. You hid behind some hay?"

I nodded, recalling the sheer terror I'd felt crammed behind those bales, waiting to be found by a large man with a gun in his waistband. Or a really shiny belt buckle. Either would have been enough to subdue me.

"How did you hide well enough that he couldn't find you?"

"If he'd kept looking, he'd have found us." I stopped and shuddered, remembering. "I was about to sneeze and had to pinch my nose shut."

"Sneeze? Isn't that kind of a cliché?"

"Totally," I said, "but my nose has no shame. When I moved, one of the boards squeaked, and a mouse ran out and he must have thought that was the squeak. Oh, and then a dog barked outside, close by. And he left."

"Well, I hate to say it, but I would have wet my pants if it had been me," Kay admitted. "Not that I'd have run off in the first place, but still."

I suddenly remembered what I'd been doing when I'd discovered the stranger going through my car. "Hey, I did find something at Bob's house." I reached into my pants pocket, which was empty. "It's in my other jeans. Hang on."

My discarded clothes lay in a damp heap on the bathroom floor. I fished the matchbook out of the pocket where I'd shoved it. It was quite wet.

"Uh oh," I said aloud.

"What?" Kay demanded. I turned to find she had followed me.

"I found this on Bob's kitchen table. A name and number are written inside, and now it's wet." I held up the matchbook.

She grabbed it and flipped it open. "Too dark here. Come on." She hurried back to stand by the living room windows. "Still readable, I think," she said, tilting it toward the light. "Luvie? Frieda?"

"Trixie," I said, taking the matchbook back. "Do you think that could be the woman in red?"

"If it is, it would certainly put a different spin on things. Let's call the number. Can you read it?"

"I think so," I said, and gave her the digits. She went to the phone on the kitchen counter.

"Tell me the number again," she commanded. She dialed, listened briefly, and made a face as she hung up.

"Busy. Damn. Hey, where's the matchbook from?"

I handed it to her. She studied it, and shook her head.

"I don't know this place," she admitted.

"Isn't the address out by the highway?"

"Yeah, near the town limits. Maybe their customers are commuters coming home from High Cross. You work all day in the city, drive most of the way back sober, and stop in for a drink when you're nearly home."

"Call them up and see if they know this Trixie," I said.

She picked up the phone again and dialed. She frowned as she listened, then hung up. "Message machine," she said. "Apparently they open at eleven a.m. and happy hour is from five to six."

"Couldn't you leave a message?"

"Yeah, but what am I going to say? Is Trixie there and did she kidnap Bob? Let me try her number again." She redialed, but the line was still busy. "Pooh. I wish she'd written an address instead of a phone number."

"Let's see if we can find the address. Fire up your computer."

Her expression brightened, and she led the way downstairs to her office. The computer was on, though the monitor had powered down. When she touched the mouse, the machine crackled and came back to life. Soon she had logged onto the Internet and typed in the phone number on a site that did reverse look ups. We both groaned at the message that there were no matches for that number.

"Yes there is," Kay groaned, "and we've got the real matches to prove it. Shoot."

"Now what?" I asked.

"Time to call the police?" She saw me shake my head. "Louisa, Bob has disappeared and you were followed by a man with a gun." I looked at her. "Well, maybe with a gun."

"I thought of something else..." My voice faltered. She gave me a quizzical look. "Well, it occurred to me that, um, maybe *Bob* wouldn't want us to call the police."

"You're the one who was so sure he isn't blackmailing anyone," she reminded me.

"Well, he's not," I maintained. I was operating purely on instinct and instinct is hard to defend. But Kay gave a slow, thoughtful nod.

"You know," she drawled, a crafty gleam beginning to shine in her eye, "if we could find out what's going on by ourselves, it would really piss off Ed."

"Do we want to piss off Ed?"

"He called you lady, didn't he? Of course we want to piss him off. Come on, it's time to ride." She hit keys to log off the computer.

"What?"

"Let's go get your car back. At least we can do that much. After that we'll figure out something else. We'll go check your phone for messages. Maybe we should do that first. No, let's get your car. Hell, maybe Bob will be back by then. I still expect him to walk in any minute."

We climbed the stairs to her apartment. "I do too. Even though I *saw* him drive off in that Mercedes, it still feels so unlikely."

108

"Let me try Trixie one more time," she said, and went to the phone.

"What about the dogs?" I asked, as she began to dial.

She paused to look at them. Emily Ann was a perfect circle on the sofa. "Bring Jack along. Maybe we'll get lucky and Bob will be home and we can give him his dog back. I'll call his place again before we leave too." She finished dialing Trixie's number, and put the receiver to her ear.

I told Emily Ann to be a good girl and that we'd be back soon.

"Still busy," Kay growled. "Let's call Bob's house. What's the number?"

I can rarely remember phone numbers, but I was able to rattle off Bob's without hesitation. As she dialed, I clipped Emily Ann's leash onto Jack's collar, since his was still in my car. He started spinning, stopping to wag when I fished a handful of chocolate chip cookies out of the Mickey Mouse cookie jar next to the flour canister. "Sorry, these are people cookies," I told him. I wrapped them in a paper towel and turned to Kay.

"No answer, just the machine," she said. "Let's go." She whirled around, yanked open the refrigerator door, and took out a bottle of water.

"What about the store?"

"I put the sign on the door saying I'd be back in an hour. No one will know what time I put it up. Rainy Tuesdays in October aren't our hottest times anyway. And what's the point of working for myself if

I can't close when I want to?"

14

We strapped on our seatbelts, and Kay took off from her parking place behind the building. Jack planted his sturdy feet between the bucket seats and leaned into the turn as she sped around the corner onto Main Street. "Tell me everything you know about Bob. Maybe it will help us figure out what's going on."

"I've told you everything already. It's not like I haven't talked to you every day." I picked up one of the cookies I had laid on the dashboard and took a bite.

She glanced at me. "I bet there's some detail you haven't told me. Just talk. Free associate."

"Okay. Um, he's tall and thin and wears plain clothing except for the All Stars." This came out thickly through the nuts and chocolate chips.

"What about his character?" She looked over her left shoulder before she changed lanes, then held out a hand. "Give me some of that. You're a whole sandwich ahead." She grabbed the cookie, chomped out a big bite, and handed it back to me.

"Yes, but I had no breakfast."

"Bob. Tell me about Bob."

111

"He's kind," was the next thing I thought of. "He talks to everyone at the dog park, even the people who are boring. He never gets impatient if someone says something dumb. And he's really good to his dog."

Kay made the turn onto Hofenstadter Boulevard and sped up to cruise past an SUV. "Ah, the most important thing about a man: how does he treat his dog. Well, you're probably right at that."

I looked over at the dog in question, who had retreated to the back seat and sat looking out the window on the driver's side. We stopped for a red light at the intersection with North Street and Kay reached for the cookie again. The movement caught Jack's attention, and he licked his lips at the sight of the cookie. It was down to a single bite, which she ate.

"All gone, Jack." The dog looked at me when I said his name, and I added in the tone one uses on funny dogs with big floppy ears, "He's just an old hungry dog, isn't he? A big old sweet hungry boy?"

Evidently 'hungry' was another word that Jack was familiar with, for he cocked his head and looked at me hopefully. I went back to my normal voice and told him, "Later, big Jack." I turned back to Kay, pushing up my glasses to rub my eyes as I thought. "Bob's also patient. He thought it was cool when I told Emily Ann to go to you at the store that first day, so we've been teaching both dogs to go back and forth between us at the park. He said he's never trained a dog before but he's really good at it. Or maybe Jack's just extra smart."

I picked up another cookie from the dashboard

as the light turned green. Kay accelerated smoothly, her right hand confident on the gear shift as she moved it through its positions until she was in fifth. I took another bite as I reached for the bottle of water. I twisted off the top and was taking a swig when I realized she had flipped on the turn signal and was slowing down.

"Where are you going? This isn't the way to Bob's house."

"I know. I just realized we could turn here and go by that bar first. Maybe Trixie will be there and we can find out what's going on and save Bob."

"You don't want to just call again?" Bars hold even less attraction for me than telephones.

"They'll have the message machine on," she said firmly, "and this will only take a few minutes. What were we talking about?"

"Bob training Jack to go to me."

"Well, you'd never trained a dog before Emily Ann either," she pointed out as we passed the next intersection.

"That's true. You should have seen Emily Ann at the park yesterday. She was playing with the other dogs and I told her to go to Bob, and she tore off to find him. He hid behind some trees when she wasn't looking and she had to search for him. She was so excited when she found him that she jumped straight up in the air."

Kay grinned as she turned onto Prairie. "That must have been a sight. Hey, maybe we could turn Jack and Emily Ann loose and tell them to go to Bob.

They could do a Lassie and find him."

"Good plan. I wish I'd thought of that last night. I could have taken Jack back to the Food Right and followed him as he unerringly sought out his master. Too bad I didn't think of it in time."

"Yeah, I don't know why you didn't," she said. A pickup changed lanes in front of us and she touched the brakes to keep from hitting it. After exhaling loudly, she went on, "It seems like you've seen Bob every day since you met."

I thought back. "That was two weeks ago yesterday. A couple of days after that I took him to the dog park for the first time, and since then we *have* seen each other at least once a day, except for Sunday. He had something else to do that day, he didn't say what. We've been to the dog park, and we went out to dinner Thursday before last. And we had breakfast with you at the Bluebird last Friday morning before we opened the store."

"He's getting to be a regular. Cleta likes him. What else?"

"We rented videos a couple of times and watched them at my house with the dogs. He went garaging with me last Saturday. He bought one of those hand-cranked juicers from the fifties because he said he had grown up with one just like it."

"Good, now you can have your orange juice freshly squeezed when you spend the night at his house."

"Kay, leave it," I commanded as though she were an errant puppy with a stolen sock in her mouth.

114

She grinned at me, unrepentant.

"So in all this time you've spent together, he's never tried to kiss you?"

"It is possible to know a man for two weeks without kissing," I informed her.

"But you've been dating. People often kiss someone they date."

"Well, we haven't. I—I didn't want to kiss him if he was going to turn out to be a reporter. And he hasn't made any moves on me, so maybe he really is a reporter and is being professional. Or he just doesn't want to kiss me."

"Ambrose says he's not gay, so it can't be that. Has he told you any more about his past? Or talked about anything he's written?"

"No. He hasn't."

We were almost out of town now. At the crossroads ahead a blinking red light glowed on and off. When we stopped, I saw that the place we were looking for was in a strip center on the left. The bar was the corner establishment, and its neighbors were a beauty parlor with a glittery handwritten sign in the window advertising Sprakle Nails. I gritted my teeth; misspelled signs make me itch. Next came an empty store front, then a double-wide shop where one could trade in used paperbacks for other used paperbacks. The business on the far end had no sign but appeared to be a lawnmower repair shop, currently not open. Maybe they were busy getting their nails sprakled. Kay turned into the parking lot and pulled up next to a dirty gray pickup that was the only vehicle in front of The Last Resort.

"Come on," she said.

"Can't I wait here for you?" Perhaps I could duck into the beauty parlor and give them a quick spelling lesson.

"No," she said firmly. "Look what happened the last time you waited in the car. Get your butt out of that seat."

I've never had any desire to frequent bars. Beyond the occasional glass of wine, I don't drink. I detest the smell of beer, and cigarette smoke makes me feel instantly emphysemic. But when Kay speaks in that tone I obey. I followed her through the front door, which was painted a dispirited dark red, into a dim and quiet cave. The jukebox in the corner was silent. A television mounted over the bar had the sound turned down to a mosquito-like buzz.

Two people watched the set. On our side of the counter a young man, probably in his late twenties, sat with his elbows on either side of an empty beer mug. His t-shirt was sleeveless and revealed a colorful dragon tattoo snaking down the length of his right arm. An elderly woman leaned on the other side of the bar, her arms folded across the bib-style apron she wore over a white t-shirt and much-washed jeans. They both looked around with mildly curious expressions when we walked in.

"Hi," Kay said. "I wonder if you could help us with something."

We made our way around a couple of tables. I noticed that the TV was tuned to a soap opera; two young and beautiful women in evening gowns were having a serious argument.

"You got car trouble?" the gray haired woman asked.

"No, no, nothing like that," Kay said, smiling. "We're trying to find someone, and we found a matchbook at his house from this place. And it had a name and phone number written inside, but the phone seems to be busy all the time."

They both stared at her. Their unsmiling expressions were so identical that I wondered if they were related.

Kay soldiered on. "Since we were driving by here, we thought we'd stop and see if you know anything about this person. The name written on the matchbook cover was Trixie. Does that ring any bells?"

The woman blinked through a too-long pause. At last she said, "Nope." Her lips closed in a thin line.

Kay tried another smile. "Are you sure?"

"It was written with purple ink," I added helpfully.

"Nope." This time she also shook her head. "Never heard of her." She turned away and focused on the television again, where a Chihuahua in a tutu now danced with an animated scrub brush.

"Oh. Well, okay. Here, let me give you my card. Just in case this Trixie should show up here again." She opened her purse, fished out one of her business cards, and laid it on the bar. Neither of them made a move to take it. The woman kept watching the screen and the man just looked at us. Finally Kay said,

"Okay. Well, thanks. Guess we'll go now."

We turned and headed for the door. Just before we reached it the young man spoke.

"Weren't you at the Food Right last night?"

I halted and turned back. "Yes. I was looking for my friend who's disappeared."

He nodded. "I heard you ask the clerk if she'd seen him."

I realized why the tattoo looked familiar. "You were buying lettuce."

He nodded. "Hope you find the guy soon."

"Uh, thanks."

He turned back to the TV, and Kay and I escaped. Jack was in the passenger seat. I pointed to the back and he hopped over. Neither of us spoke until we were back in the car. Kay turned the key, and as the engine fired up she looked over at me and started laughing.

"Good lord, Louisa, was that weird or what?" She looked over her shoulder and backed out of the parking space.

"Any event that includes a Chihuahua in a tutu is weird."

"You saw that guy at the grocery store?"

"Yeah. I recognized the tattoo but I couldn't think where I'd seen it."

"Did he act suspicious at the store? Could he be involved in Bob's disappearance, do you think?" She pulled onto the street, heading back towards Bob's house.

"I only saw him for a few seconds in the produce

aisle. Unless he'd been picking out that lettuce for at least half an hour, I don't see how he could even have been in the store when Bob was there."

"It just seems like a huge coincidence," she insisted.

I nodded. "I know, but on the other hand the Food Right is the only big grocery store on this end of town."

"True. Did you believe them, about not knowing who Trixie is?"

"I have no idea." I thought about it. "The place is small enough that you'd think they would know their clientele, but Trixie may not be a regular. For all we know she was only in the place once. Or maybe she's never been there. Maybe Bob stopped in and picked up the matches and met Trixie somewhere else."

"Has Bob ever suggested taking you to a bar?"

I shook my head. "No. And I've only seen him drink a glass of wine with dinner. I don't think he's the bar type."

"Trixie might not even be her name. I mean, who's named Trixie?"

"We just don't have any information to go on, other than the name, false or not, and phone number," I complained.

She nodded. "True." She drove in silence for a block, then sighed. "I suppose it would have been too easy to find Trixie at the bar and have her tell us what's going on."

"I know, but it would have been nice."

119

"Hey, get my phone out of my purse and call her number again."

I fished around in her bag and found the tiny instrument. It flipped open easily enough, but required some surreptitious poking at its buttons to get a dial tone. I was embarrassed to let her see how little I had used one of these devices. I finally punched in the number that by now I had memorized.

"Still busy," I reported.

She scowled. "Dammit, how can anyone talk that long? She must be the original motormouth."

We passed the parking lot where last night I'd watched a woman in red take Bob to a gray Mercedes and drive away.

"This is where it all started," I commented, and Kay glanced over at the store.

"Right. Hey, that's the store with the weird music. Maybe they were just fleeing from that."

Remembering what I'd heard when I went inside to look for Bob last night, I said, "That's the most plausible thing we've come up with yet."

She reached over and patted my leg. "Look, maybe we'll get lucky and he'll be home by now, and we can find out what's going on," she said.

"Are you sure it's okay just to drive up to his house? What if that guy is still ransacking my car?"

"Louisa, he was through with the ransacking when he headed for the house. And why would he hang around after you got away? It'll be fine. We'll just go see if Bob's come back, and pick up your car and—"

Since passing the Food Right we'd been following the route I'd taken earlier that morning. As we neared the turnoff to Bob's house I saw something by the other side of the road. "Oh my god!" I grabbed Kay's arm. "Don't stop, keep going. Do not turn into Bob's driveway!"

The car rocked as she pulled out of my grasp. Kay looked around wildly but kept driving. "What? What?"

"The Mercedes! The gray Mercedes! It's parked off the road back there!"

15

Kay looked over her shoulder, making the car swerve. "What! Where?"

"Watch the road." I poked her in the ribs. She slapped at my hand but returned to driving mode.

"I can turn around up here," she said. No other cars were in sight. She did a three point turn, and drove slowly back. "Where's this car?"

"It's pulled off the road by those bushes."

"How do you know it's the same one?" she asked. "Must be a zillion gray Mercedes around." She pulled off the road onto the shoulder a few yards beyond the Mercedes.

"Of this vintage? Don't you think that's pushing coincidence a little far?" I retorted. "Last night one carries Bob off to god knows where, and today one just like it is hidden near his house. You figure the odds."

"It's not really hidden, it's just inconspicuously parked," she hedged.

I snorted. "Pretty inconspicuous. You didn't notice it."

"Let's go check it out." Jack slithered into her abandoned seat when she got out. "You stay in the car, Jack, honey," she said. "We'll be right back."

A graveled shoulder and a drainage ditch bordered the road, and a few feet away barbed wire fencing kept whatever might be lurking off the road. A pickup truck traveling about eighty miles an hour thundered past us, flinging a piece of rock that hit me in the knee. I yelped, but Kay didn't notice. She looked in the passenger-side window of the Mercedes and tried the door.

"Locked," she muttered. "Try the driver's door."

"It's locked too," I reported.

"Damn. I should have learned something practical like how to pick a car lock instead of all that art history. Look, there's a map on the passenger seat."

Nothing else of interest could be seen in the car. It had nice leather upholstery that precisely matched the gray exterior, and the steering wheel was wrapped in what looked like red suede. I walked around and peered in at the map. "It looks like a local map," I said, and Kay nodded.

"Which could mean that your woman in red has never been to Bob's house before, assuming that this is indeed her car," she said.

"Look out, Nancy Drew," I commented. My knee hurt where the rock had hit it. I leaned over to rub the sore spot.

She walked all the way around the Mercedes

and paused to inspect the license plate. "Hmmm, I wonder if this is a rental plate."

"Right, probably, I know I always rent a car when I'm planning to kidnap someone." She raised her chin at me but I went on. "Anyway, aren't rental cars always compact Fords? And aren't they always white? Where would you rent a car this old?"

"It is perfectly possible to rent a Mercedes," she said haughtily.

"It's awfully clean," I said. "Cleaner than yours. Maybe it spent the night in a garage somewhere."

"Thank you, Ms. Sherlock." Abruptly she turned away from the Mercedes and headed back toward her own car. As she did, a battered old Volkswagen bug slowed down.

"You ladies need any help?" called the driver, who appeared to be about nineteen, with blazing red hair standing up in a ring around his extravagantly freckled face.

Kay gave him a wave and a big grin. "No, thanks. We're just fine, but you are so sweet to ask." He waved back and gunned his engine, grinding gears. By the time I limped back to Kay's car the Volkswagen was out of sight. Jack was still on the driver's seat. "You planning on taking over the driving?" Kay asked him. His tail whipped. "You're not old enough for a license. Hop in back, that's a good boy." He obeyed, and we got in. Kay checked for traffic and put the gear shift into first.

"Wait a minute," I said. "You're not going back to Bob's driveway, are you?"

"Well, yeah." Her tone was impatient.

"No! We have no idea if that woman came here alone or with Bob, or if she has someone else with her. I mean, she's probably in cahoots with that guy—"

"Cahoots?" She raised an eyebrow at me.

"—and she may have used a weapon to make Bob go with her. And I still think the guy searching my car had a gun. We could get shot. Or they might shoot Bob. Maybe now is when we should call the police."

"Not till we see if anyone is at Bob's house. Okay, we'll go through the woods."

I couldn't suppress a groan. She gave me a look. "Okay, okay, you're right," I said, holding up my hands in surrender. "I'm the one who doesn't want to drive up to the house. Go about a mile and make a right."

Kay pulled onto the road and sped back the way we'd come. In a couple of minutes we entered the housing tract. Jack's feet were planted on the console again, and his long ear brushed my arm as he leaned into the turn.

"I have no idea how to get to the old road that leads to that barn," I told her.

"At least we're not on foot this time," she said, and turned right. "And it's not raining." She turned right again, followed the curve of the street around to the left, then took the next right. The road to the barn was just ahead, leading into a stand of trees.

"I can't believe it was that simple," I said.

"I figured it had to be on the western edge of the tract. Maybe we can drive it. How muddy was it earlier?" Kay asked.

I peered at the track, trying to remember how squishy it had been. "I don't know," I said. "I was too busy being wet myself to pay attention to the ground."

"Let's try. If it's too soft for the car we'll walk."

She shifted into low gear and turned onto the old road. We'd gone about three hundred yards when the back wheels whined in a spin and the car fishtailed.

"Oops. Let me back up and we'll walk from here." She eased the car back to firmer ground. "Okay, let's go."

"Will your car be okay? What if someone needs to drive through?"

Kay paused in the act of opening the car door to turn and look at me. "Lou, look at this road, if you want to call it that. I'm not real concerned about traffic here."

She was right, of course. I swung open the car door and levered myself out onto the still wet ground. "Okay, it's this way. I have no idea how far."

She pressed the button on her car remote to lock the doors, slung her purse over her shoulder, and struck off at a good pace, paying no attention to the wet grass that slapped at her legs. I've never understood how someone who is three inches shorter than me can walk so fast.

Jack and I followed. After a few steps I paused to free him from the leash. I stuffed it into my fanny pack as I hurried to catch up with Kay.

Just as finding the track to the barn had been a

matter of two or three turns, it seemed to take no time at all to come into view of the barn itself. As we approached, the clouds parted and a ray of sunlight turned the building to gleaming silver. Kay paused to look at it. "It's certainly picturesque," she commented. "I wonder who owns it. Too bad it's so out of the way, you could really do something with a building like that."

I remembered how scary that barn had been while I was hiding behind some hay bales from a big man with a gun. Or a shiny belt. "I could really do something with my car, too," I said firmly, and kept going past her. She sped up and passed me. Jack bounced between us.

Kay approached the lower level of the barn and reached for the door. Suddenly Jack threw his head back and sniffed the air. He gave one loud bay and charged around the right side of the building. "Jack!" I hissed. "Come back!" I hurried after him, scrambling to climb the hill the barn was built into. When I rounded the corner to the back of the barn, Jack was at the door, sniffing and digging at the ground in front of it.

"What's up, Jack?" I said. I couldn't see anything different from earlier that day. Jack put his nose to the crack where the door met the frame and inhaled deeply, then pushed at the door with a paw.

I hesitated. "What if—" but before I could think of a what-if Kay had shouldered past me and pulled the door open. Jack was inside in a flash. Kay and I paused just inside the door for our eyes to adjust to the relative darkness. But Jack went straight for the pile of hay bales where we had hidden and nosed something sticking out from behind them.

A foot.

A foot in a canvas high top basketball shoe.

A black canvas high top basketball shoe.

16

I couldn't have moved if I'd been poked with an electric cattle prod. My brain was seized with terror. I saw that foot and everything else faded into blackness.

Jack was not similarly afflicted. He let out one eerie, high pitched, strangled cry, his whole body thrashed into a wag, and he disappeared behind the hay bales where the body lay.

The shoe moved, rolling over from toe down to toe up. A groan. Major rustling of hay. Jack uttered a long howling moan.

"Help, I'm being attacked by a tongue," came Bob's voice.

Kay flew across the rough boards of the floor. I discovered I could breathe again, and even move. I hurried after her.

Bob looked up from his cocoon of hay bales and grinned. The navy sweater was gone; otherwise he wore last night's clothes. His face, ears, and neck were being thoroughly scrubbed by Jack's long pink tongue. I leaned over and grabbed Jack's collar and pulled him backwards, then held on as he bucked and wiggled to get back to Bob.

Kay reached down and offered her hand to Bob, who took it and pulled himself upright.

"Ladies," he said by way of greeting, nodding and brushing off wisps of hay. He looked very tired and rumpled and altogether wonderful. I let go of Jack's collar and threw my arms around him. Immediately his long arms wrapped around me, and we clung to each other, my face buried against his flannel shirt.

We were blasted apart by Jack.

"Whoa, Jack," Bob said. "Easy, boy." He knelt and began to scratch Jack down the spine.

I opened my mouth to say something—I have no idea what—but Kay was faster. "Bob," she exclaimed, "where the hell have you been? How did you get here? How long have you been here? What is going on? Lou has been worried sick about you!"

He looked up at me over the wiggling dog. "This is the damnedest mess," he said, "and I don't want to get you involved in it. You saw me get carted off from the store last night?"

I nodded. "In a gray Mercedes like the one sitting out on the road a few yards from your driveway."

"What?" Bob stood up. Jack sat down on his foot.

"Yeah, we saw it just now," Kay said, conveniently forgetting that she hadn't seen it at all until I

130

pointed it out. "That's why we came through the woods, we're sneaking up on your house to get Lou's car back."

He crossed to the door and peered out. "Your car, Louisa?" he said. He gave me a quick look over his shoulder before resuming his inspection of the woods.

"I went to your house early this morning to see if you were there, and while I was inside I looked out and a man was searching my car. Jack was scared so we took off through the woods and made our way to Kay's store. Now we're coming to get my car back."

Bob turned back to look at us. "I need to find out what's going on at my house." His voice was crisp with command. "Kay, you take Louisa and Jack back to your car and I'll—"

"No way, buster," she broke in. "We're not leaving you to disappear again. Louisa and I are coming with you."

"You can't—" He stopped. The identical stony expressions on our faces said clearly that we would not be left behind. "Okay, okay, we'll all go," he said, throwing his hands in the air. Then he grinned at us. "Come on, we'd better hurry."

17

The three of us—and Jack—peered cautiously out of the barn door, scanning the surrounding woods for any lurking bad guys. Bob slipped out and held the door for Kay and me. He closed the door quietly and headed off at a quick pace with Kay and Jack right behind him. I brought up the rear. He must have spent some time in these woods, because he went straight to a path that let us proceed without being mauled by the surrounding vegetation. He moved swiftly and silently. No barbed wire got in the way.

Of course they both walked faster than me, getting further and further ahead. I felt my tension grow with each step. Why hadn't I insisted we call the police when we found the gray Mercedes? I should have just ignored being called 'lady' in a sarcastic tone. Captain Johnson's annoying professional opinion shouldn't have stopped me, nor Kay's desire to outmaneuver an ex-boyfriend.

What if the woman who had kidnapped Bob was still there? Or the guy who'd searched my car—or both? And what if they were armed and saw us and started shooting? What if he hadn't just been searching the car but had planted a bomb? Or they had filled the house with poison gas and when we went in we were all killed? What if they really were space aliens and all this was taking place on another planet where they had whisked us in our sleep so they could observe how humans react under pressure?

"What if you stop making up stupid scenarios and catch up with Kay and Bob," I muttered out loud.

Kay was nearly out of sight. I picked up my pace until I was nearly trotting, which is no more comfortable on foot than on the back of a horse. I didn't see the large stick in the path in front of me, and my foot came down squarely on it. It rolled, throwing me off balance. I lurched and walked into an enormous spider web stretched between two bushes. Fortunately it was untenanted, but its sticky tendrils clung to my face. I shuddered as I batted it off, making involuntary ugh noises.

By the time I caught up, the others were at the edge of the woods overlooking Bob's house. Kay crouched behind some bushes, and Bob lurked behind a big tree a few feet away. I knelt beside Kay, hoping the shrubbery was big enough to provide cover for us both. "What's going on?" I hissed.

"We're waiting to see if the coast is clear," Kay whispered back.

"Well, we can't see that from down here," I said,

and pushed myself back to my feet. I hunched over so I could see through the screen of branches but not be seen from the house. I hoped. The underbrush rustled, and Jack came snuffling towards me. "Jack, down," I hissed sternly. He looked surprised but dropped to his belly.

From here I could see the back and one side of Bob's house. Beyond that my car still sat between the house and the garage. The only sounds were the breeze making its way through the underbrush, a couple of blue jays squabbling over something, and a rushing sound I thought was the nearby river, but might have been traffic on the road. Under other circumstances it would have been wonderfully peaceful, but I was so tense the scene seemed like a horror movie, just before something jumps out and devours some of the characters.

Kay scrambled to her feet and looked back and forth between Bob and the house. I decided the place was deserted and straightened up to ease the kink in my back. A single loud bang had Jack on his feet and surprised a loud squeak out of one of us. Me, I think. My first mental image was of large shotguns, before I remembered that Bob's screen door made exactly that sound when it slammed shut. A hurrying form appeared from the front of the house, her back to us. The woman in red. Though she was now dressed in jeans and a red plaid shirt. She went straight to my car., She peered through the driver's side window, shading her eyes with one hand. Then she opened the door and slid in behind the wheel. I heard the engine start. The blonde pulled the car door shut, backed around until she was headed for the road, gunned the engine, and drove away.

"My car! She's stolen my car!" I yelped, heedless of being overheard.

"Louisa, did you leave your keys in the car?" Bob asked.

I grimaced and gave a nod. "I thought I'd only be in your house for a few minutes."

Beside me Kay scrabbled in her purse. She pulled out her tiny phone and dialed. "Police? Oh, Kerry Sue, it's you. This is Kay. Yeah, I'm okay, but...No, I didn't call for Ed. No, I need to report a stolen car...Of course I'm not kidding... No, it's not my car, it belongs to my...Yes, but...Listen, this car is being stolen right now, I mean this very minute. I'm watching it being driven...If you put out a call right now someone could—"

She listened to the chirps that were Kerry Sue, sighed, folded the phone and looked at us. "Well, it's business as usual down at the cop shop. That was Kerry Sue Maddock, undoubtedly the stupidest person in town, so naturally they gave her the job of dispatcher. She said they're kind of busy right now and told me to call back in ten minutes."

18

Bob straightened to his full height and gave Kay a puzzled look. His expression was that of a man trying to translate words into a language he understood. "The police told you to call back?"

"Not exactly," she said. "Kerry Sue told me to call back. Well, okay, yes, she does work for the police, but she's not *of* the police, if you know what I mean."

His furrowed brow indicated that he did not.

"Bob," I said, "have you lived in a small town before?"

"No. Not as small as Willow Falls, anyway. Just when I was in college."

"College doesn't count," I told him. "A lot of things happen in small towns because of who you are. Kerry Sue being the police dispatcher is one of them. I can give you her genealogy later."

"Okay, if you say so," he replied. "Anyway, let's go down to the house and—"

"No!" Kay and I barked the word in unison. We looked at each other. I let her continue.

"It's not safe," she said. "You're mixed up in something, and the other side knows where you live."

"True," he agreed. "So what do you suggest?"

"Would they have any reason to connect you to me?"

"I don't think so," he said. "Unless they've been following me for a while. But merely following me is probably not their agenda."

"The phone message," I said. Kay and Bob looked at me. I hurried on. "I came here last night to get Jack, and someone had left a message on your phone—you'd been spotted and should be careful."

"I think I know who was. Did they leave a name?"

I shook my head. "They started talking before the recording began."

"Well, at least let me go listen to that," Bob said.

"Um, you can't," I told him. "It—it got erased."

Sudden amusement sprang to his eyes but he didn't say anything.

"Anyway," Kay jumped back in, "they know where you live, and they probably don't know where I live, and I have fresh bagels and cream cheese and the last of the summer tomatoes in my fridge."

"Food?" said Bob. He suddenly looked exhausted.

"Food," Kay assured him. And with one more glance at Bob's house, we turned to retrace our steps to Kay's car.

Emily Ann flowed off the couch and over to Bob. She placed her front paws on his shoulders and touched his cheek delicately with her nose.

"Thank you, Emily Ann," he said quietly. She gazed into his eyes before settling back onto the floor.

Kay walked straight into the kitchen, opened the refrigerator, and started hauling out the promised victuals. "I don't know about you all," she threw over her shoulder, "but having adventures always makes me ravenous. And Louisa ate my cookies in the car."

"We both ate them. And I didn't have any breakfast."

"Let's get some food and after that, Bob has major explaining to do."

We had postponed his explanations until now. He'd set a quick pace back through the woods, and it was hard to carry on conversation between the front and back seats in the car. While she drove, Kay had continued trying to report my stolen vehicle. First the phone had rung and rung until she clicked it off, shaking her head. The next attempt was answered, but Kerry Sue must have stepped away from the phone. After an initial "Hello?" I heard Kay's voice take on a frosty tone.

"Ah, Ed...yes, this is Kay..." She checked her mirrors, pulled the car over to the curb and killed the engine. "Well, in spite of what that idiot Kerry Sue Maddock might have said, I am most definitely *not* calling to see how you are. I know how you are, remember? Which I why you and I are no longer seeing each other...Yes, of course you do, I'd never argue with that...yes, my cousin has everything to do with the fact that I'm calling you—" She drummed her fingers on the steering wheel and hunched her shoulders. The atmosphere in the car began to feel close and I tried to roll down my window, but with the engine turned off the electric button wouldn't work. I thought longingly of the simple hand cranks in my own car.

"Did Kerry Sue happen to mention that I have called three times because my cousin's car was stolen? Yes, stolen...The first time I called we were watching the woman drive Louisa's car away. You could have caught her by now, which I happen to know would have looked good in your monthly report to the city council...No, that is *not* a threat— I can't talk to you. Here, talk to Louisa." With a face like thunder she thrust the phone in my direction. I took it gingerly and held it to my ear, but I must have hit one of its miniscule buttons and disconnected it, for all I heard was a dial tone.

"Um, I guess I cut him off." I glanced at Kay for help but she was looking away from me out her side window. I was still trying to find the right button to make the thing work when the phone gave the annoying rendition of Fur Elise that Kay had selected for its ring. I fumbled with it. "Hello?"

"Hello? Mrs. McGuire? We seemed to have been disconnected." It was Chief Johnson, sounding as frosty as Kay. "I understand that your car has been stolen? Can you give me the particulars?"

"It was the woman who drove away with Bob last night—"

"What?" His voice rose several notes. "The same woman has stolen your car? What about Mr. Richardson? Was he still with her?"

"No, we found him in the old barn, and we were going to his house to get my car, and we arrived just in time to see her drive off in it. She was wearing different clothes, but it was definitely the same woman." Something about the man made me babble.

Silence stretched into several seconds. When he spoke his voice seemed carefully controlled. "And is Mr. Richardson all right?"

"Yes, thank you, he's okay," I replied. "Do you want to speak to—" Bob's hand gripped my shoulder over the back of the seat, and when I looked at him he shook his head urgently. "—um, to Kay again?" I finished, making a puzzled face at Bob. Now Kay shook her head and scowled at me.

"No, that won't be necessary. Just give me the information on your car and we'll start looking for it."

I described my little car's make and color.

"That sounds like the car you were driving last night."

"Yes, Bob and I have identical cars. Well, except for the license plates."

"I see." He managed to infuse his words with the suggestion that it was extremely peculiar for Bob and me to have the same kind of car. "All right, give me the plate number for yours."

I did, thinking it was a miracle I was able to

remember it.

"How was she able to just drive off in your car?"

I knew this was going to come up. "I left the keys in it." At least I hadn't babbled this time.

"I see." Several more seconds ticked by. "And the theft occurred at Mr. Richardson's house? All right, we'll get on it. I take it you no longer need to file a missing person report."

"No, he's not missing now, thank you."

"Right. That's the usual pattern in these cases." He disconnected the call. I pulled the phone away from my ear to look at it. The usual pattern? How many men disappeared out of grocery stores in this town? I knew that Willow Falls had changed in the years I'd been away, but still. I handed the phone back to Kay, who dropped it into the compartment between our seats and restarted the car.

"He said they'd look for my car."

"Great," she growled as she pulled back onto the street. Brakes screeched, a horn like the trumpet of doom blared, and an enormous SUV pulled around us. Several teenage faces glared from the windows. "Damn. I'm going to get us all killed, and you can lay that on Ed's doorstep."

Now, back in her apartment, Kay bustled about toasting bagels, spreading cream cheese, and slicing tomatoes, while I poured tea over ice into tall glasses. Bob excused himself to wash up. When he returned we each grabbed a plate and glass and settled at the trestle table. Bob took a huge bite.

"Thanks, Kay, I'm really hungry," he said.

She too had taken a bite. She said thickly, "I thought you would be." She swallowed. "Okay, you can have your bagel. After that I want to know what's going on."

He nodded, taking another bite. He seemed to have aged several years since yesterday. I looked down at the food on my plate. I wasn't sure what would happen if I tried to eat. My stomach was as confused as my head. A few hours ago, all I had wanted was to know that Bob was safe. Now he was back, and I dreaded what I might hear in the next few minutes. What, after all, did I know about this man? He could be anyone. Or anything. He could be the reporter I'd been dreading, or a spy or in the witness protection program or a hit man or—

"Okay." Bob put down his glass of tea. "This is hard to say, it sounds so insane. I mean, stuff like this doesn't happen to people like me, only it has, and—"

"Just *tell* us," Kay broke in sternly.

"Yes. Right. Well, the beginning of it was, I found out about a murder."

I had just managed a sip of tea, which caught in my throat. I snorted and Kay whacked me on the back. "I'm okay," I said, shaking her off. "I'm okay. Go on."

"There's so much you don't know about me. First of all, I'm not a writer. It felt so weird to lie about that." Bob shook his head. "I was sure you could tell by my expression I was making it up, Louisa. When I met you it was the first time I tried out any of the cover story I'd made up."

Aha! put in one of my mental voices. You were

right about him hiding something. "I was afraid you were a reporter looking for a story on how my husband died," I blurted.

"A reporter? No, I said I was a writer to have an excuse not to go to a job every day."

"What the hell are you, then?" Kay demanded. "Is Bob Richardson your real name?"

"Yes. Really. Coming up with fake ID was beyond my capabilities. I'm a hypnotherapist." We both stared at him. He gave us a faint smile. "Well, somebody has to do it," he quipped.

"I saw a website for a hypnotist with that name," Kay said.

I nodded, remembering the website as well. "And an artist and a guy who breeds water lilies," I added. Kay gave me her 'too much information' look.

"I do have a website," Bob said. "I'm pretty well known in High Cross. I've done hypnosis a long time, over twenty years. I work with all kinds of patients, but my specialty is hypnotic anesthesia."

"Is what?" Kay asked.

"Hypnotic anesthesia. Some people are allergic to drugs or they don't want to use them. If they're capable of being deeply hypnotized, we can use it as an alternative to regular anesthesia during an operation or at the dentist, or during childbirth. It can speed healing too."

He picked up his glass of iced tea and drank the last of it. He stared at the ice, then rose and walked over to the pitcher sitting on the kitchen counter.

"A few months ago I started working with a

new patient, Ian. Nineteen, planning to be a chef. Just starting at the culinary academy in High Cross. Nice kid, very focused on what he wanted to do." He refilled his glass and stared at it as he spoke. "He needed to have his wisdom teeth pulled, and he was allergic to most anesthetics. We had some sessions to establish his ability to go into deep trance and he was a good subject.

"I was testing the depth of his trance when something new came up. By regressing a patient in time, taking him back to his last birthday and having him recall details, and repeating it for the year before, I can get a good idea how deeply hypnotized he is. I use birthdays since they have special significance to most people. But when we reached Ian's fifteenth birthday it was clear that something happened on that day. He became agitated. I pulled him away from it to relax and to give myself time to think."

Bob put his glass down on the counter to pace about the room. "Unexpected reactions do come up when you hypnotize people, and it's part of my job to help them over rough spots in their lives if I can. Sometimes they come to me with what they think is their problem, but deep down they need to deal with something else, something that's too hard to look at directly. Of course you have to be very, very careful that you're not influencing the patient to create false memories that seem real." He paused to look at us, then resumed his restless pacing. "Ian's reaction to his fifteenth birthday was so intense that I wondered whether we should keep going. But I've worked with

144

hundreds of people, and I believed I could help him get over whatever had happened to him."

The pacing brought Bob to the window that overlooks the alley behind the store. He stood looking out, the light bleaching out the normal laugh lines by his eyes. His shoulders sagged.

"I made sure Ian was still in a deep trance, and had him distance himself from what he was describing, as though it were a movie he was watching rather than something that was happening to him," Bob said. He turned away from the window and began pacing again. "I took him back to when he woke up on that day. His dog woke him up. It was on the bed next to him, growling. He looked at the clock by his bed and saw it was 3:17. He got up and went to the door and saw his stepfather coming out of the master bedroom. Ian and his stepfather did not get along at all, and his dog positively hated the man, which explained the growling. So Ian went back to bed."

Bob paced to the kitchen counter and picked up his glass of tea, returned to the table and sat down. Jack came and laid his muzzle on Bob's lap. Bob lifted one of the soft black ears and let it fall through his fingers.

"Ian said when he woke up again, it was late morning. The house was quiet. He went down to the kitchen and let his dog out. He was surprised that his mother wasn't up. She always made a fuss about his birthday breakfast. So he went upstairs to wake her."

Bob paused to sip a little tea. "This is when his demeanor changed, and I had to remind him he was a spectator, that he was watching a movie. He said the boy crossed the room. The mother was alone in the bed, and she was very still. He saw that she wasn't breathing. An empty pill bottle sat on the bedside table. Ian said the boy reached out and picked up the bottle and looked at it. Set it down again. The boy was saying, mom, mom, oh mom, no. He ran out of the room and dialed nine one one and sat in the kitchen crying until the paramedics and the police arrived."

Kay looked over at me with an expression of concern. A couple of tears had escaped and were running down my face. I shook my head at her and wiped the tears away, but more followed them. I rose and left the room, going to the bathroom for some tissue.

Behind me I heard Bob say, "What's wrong with Louisa?"

"Her—her mother died a few months ago," Kay replied.

"Yes, I remember she said she'd inherited her house."

"She probably didn't tell you her mother committed suicide." Kay sounded resolutely matter of fact.

"No, she left out that part," Bob said. "I'm so sorry. I didn't mean to say anything—"

I blew my nose hard and missed part of what Kay was saying, tuning back in to hear, "...weren't close, but it was still upsetting. She'll be all right."

I honked into the tissue again, made a face at myself in the bathroom mirror, and went back to the table. "I'm okay," I said. "I just needed a little time out." Emily Ann rose from the couch and walked over, ducked under the table, and lay down on my feet; I felt comforted to my bones. "Go on, Bob, what else did Ian say?"

Bob gave me an anxious look before continuing, "Ian had been through enough, so again I distanced him from his memories, brought him forward to the present and woke him. He was relaxed, a little sleepy. I said I'd taken him back through his birthdays, and that it appeared he had suffered trauma on his fifteenth. In an instant he went from relaxed to looking sick. He said should have warned me, that one was really bad. He didn't remember much about that day, and he was curious about what he had told me. I began to repeat what he'd said, starting with seeing his stepfather in the middle of the night, and he stopped me. He said he couldn't have seen his stepfather that night because he was out of town, and that the police had checked up on where he'd been because he inherited a lot of money from Ian's mother. I offered to let him watch the video of his session—"

"Video?" I broke in.

Bob looked at me and nodded. "I tape every session. Protection in case someone accuses you of unprofessional conduct while they were hypnotized. Or sometimes people want to know what they said or how they acted. There's nothing secret about it, the camera is in plain sight and all my patients know about it. I give them a copy of the tape if they're uncomfortable with anything. I don't want anyone's session to be a secret from them. Anyway, Ian wouldn't watch the tape. He got up and said he had to go. He looked like he was about to cry." He stopped and put his hands on top of the table and looked across the room, then back at us. "I never saw him again."

He pushed himself up from his chair and started pacing again. "I left a couple of days later to go to a conference, and when I got back I happened to see Ian's dentist, the one who was doing his wisdom teeth. We talked for a couple of minutes, and I asked him when Ian's surgery was scheduled, and he looked at me like I was from another planet. He said it had been in the papers that Ian had killed himself a few days before."

He stopped pacing. His face was grim. "What he said was, he committed suicide 'just like his mother did a few years ago.'"

Silence hovered around us. After a few moments Bob went on. "I know it's not proof of anything. But I'm sure that Ian *did* see his stepfather leaving his mother's room the night she died. I know he was upset by remembering his fifteenth birthday. But unless he changed completely after he left my office, he wasn't despondent. He'd already weathered the trauma of finding his mother dead, and had been able to go on with his life. I didn't see anything in several sessions with him to suggest he was depressed or was considering suicide. He had made peace with his past and was working toward his future, not thinking about ending it. But he was dead. I was convinced that Ian and his mother had both been murdered, she for her money and he because he knew too much."

Kay shifted restlessly in her seat. "Seems like

some piece of evidence somewhere would put the stepfather on the scene. They couldn't have had anyone like Ed investigating the case."

I stared at her. *Like Ed?* But she was still talking.

"You haven't told us about the woman in red. Why were you kidnapped? And how did you get away? And why the heck did she steal Louisa's car?"

He came back to the table and sat down again. "The tape," he said. "I think they're looking for the tape of my hypnosis session with Ian. His stepfather's whole life depends on no one suspecting he's killed two people. The tape isn't proof of anything but he must be desperate not to have questions asked in the wrong places. You're right, Kay. If he murdered them, some bit of incriminating evidence could exist—or he's afraid it does. And if he's killed twice, I don't think he'd hesitate to go for three. The safest thing seemed for me to get out of town for a while."

"So his stepfather knew that Ian was seeing you and being hypnotized?" I asked.

Bob shook his head. "I don't know. I didn't think so at the time. Ian was still living at home while he went to school, but I can't imagine them discussing anything. Everything he said about his stepfather indicated animosity between them. Of course, that's not unusual between parents and kids, especially stepparents. I believe it was his aunt who recommended that he try a hypnotist, apparently she used one some time ago."

Kay frowned. "If the stepfather didn't know Ian

149

was seeing you, let alone that you taped his recollection of the night his mother died, how the hell did he connect you to Ian?"

"Ian may have confronted him with his recovered memory. Or maybe something just came out about him going to a hypnotist. I have no idea if he revealed my name, but there aren't a whole lot of hypnotists in High Cross. Or someone in the police department could have told his stepfather I have the tape. Or he found out I stole Ian's dog."

19

I stared at Jack. "You stole him? Jack was *Ian's* dog?" I asked at the same time Kay blurted, "The police told him?"

Bob patted his lap with one hand and Jack reared up to put his front paws there. Bob rubbed a finger along the top of his long nose. "I had to, he was starving," he answered me first. "After I heard that Ian was dead, I didn't know what to do. I thought of nothing else for days. If I hadn't hypnotized him, he might never have recovered that memory and would be alive."

"He came to you for help, and you did your best," I consoled.

"I know, but...I can't tell you how bad that feels. I decided I had to go to the police with my suspicions."

"The High Cross police?" Kay asked.

151

Bob nodded. "I made an appointment with a detective. It was awful. The whole time I was explaining, he kept shaking his head. He seemed to think hypnosis is a parlor game and that I had as much credibility as someone who sends out those spam emails about hypnotizing women into bed. I'll never forget his voice when he asked me where the tape with this so-called information was. He told me to bring him the tape, and that he'd check into it, but I was sure the whole thing was headed straight for the round file."

"Where is the tape?" I asked.

"It was in my safety deposit box at the bank. Anyway, I left the police station angry. I thought I could put it in their laps and be done with it, that they'd immediately start an investigation. Now I was more frustrated than ever."

"Yeah, some cops can really drive you nuts." Kay was scowling, and I didn't think it was because of the High Cross police.

Bob continued, "I drove around trying to decide what to do. I had a copy of the tape that I could take to them. My gut feeling was to keep the original, which had Ian's signature on the label. But that detective had made me uneasy. I can't explain it. He was just way more negative than he needed to be."

"Maybe he's just used to playing the bad cop role," I put in.

"Could be, who knows. Anyway, I found myself driving up in the hills and realized that Ian's house was somewhere close by. I circled around until I found the right street. Now I felt stupid. I hadn't driven by someone's house since I was sixteen and borrowed my parents' car to cruise by some girl's house. Just on the off chance she'd be on her front steps to appreciate how cool I was at the wheel of a '66 Fairlane." He shook his head and smiled a little.

"Ian's house, when I found it, had about an acre of grass in front. The only thing out of place was this black lump in the shade of one of the bushes near the street. I slowed down and the lump moved. It lifted its head and looked at me, and my foot stomped on the brake. You've never seen anything so pitiful. He stood up as soon as I stopped, and he was skin and bones. Ian's stepfather must have kicked him out of the house and left him."

"Maybe he'd dumped him somewhere and Jack had made his way back," I said.

"Hmmm, his paw pads were pretty worn, that could be it. Anyway, I didn't think, I just leaned over and opened the passenger door. I called him, and he wobbled over to the car and climbed in and we drove away."

"Jeez, this is a really bad man," I blurted. Kay and Bob looked at me and I felt myself blushing. "Well, two murders are bad enough, but to starve poor Jack…" My voice trailed off, but Kay was nodding.

"Yeah, and I bet he did it all for money he was enjoying anyway, since he was married to Ian's mother," she said. "I wonder if she was going to divorce him or something. But Bob, I still want to know what happened when you got picked up last night. Who is that woman and where does she fit in?"

153

"And how you got away," I added.

"Oh, that." Bob said. "Well, to start at the end, I hypnotized her into bed."

20

"What!" Kay and I yelped together.

He remained deadpan for a moment, then grinned. "Okay, not what you're thinking. I hypnotized her and she fell asleep. It took a while but I was able to wiggle out of the rope she had tied me up with. So I left."

"On foot?" Kay asked.

"Yeah. Unfortunately she fell asleep with her head on her purse, and she'd put my wallet inside. I was afraid I'd wake her if I tried to get it back, so I didn't have any money to call a cab to get back home. Her car keys were in there too, so I couldn't take that. Plus I wasn't sure where it was safe to go."

"I wish I'd been there to see it," Kay commented. "You make it sound awfully easy."

"I'd say she had been hypnotized before. She was very suggestible. She must have been tired anyway, and once it got late it was fairly simple to put her into a trance and suggest that she have a good, long sleep."

"Good grief," I said, "can you do that with anyone? Hypnotize them without them knowing?" I could feel every paranoid instinct I'd ever had flaring to new life.

"No, no, of course I can't. And I wouldn't have done it to her if I hadn't been desperate." He looked me in the eyes. "I promise you I would never do something like that to you. I doubt if I could."

Our gaze stayed locked until Kay broke in. "How about going back to the beginning? At least our beginning, or rather Louisa's. Who *is* the woman who kidnapped you?"

Bob turned to face her. "That's the weird thing, Kay, I don't know. I have no idea who she is or where she fits into the picture. She had a gun—that's how she got me out of the grocery store. You remember I went in for dog food, Louisa?"

I nodded. "I was listening to the radio and the next thing I knew you came out with this blonde and got into another car. I half killed myself getting into the driver's seat to follow you. If you ever lock the door when I'm waiting in the car again I may shoot you myself."

His eyes crinkled in a smile. "I'll try to break myself of the habit," he promised. "I wanted you to be safe."

"She was safer than you, anyway," Kay said.

"True. So I was in the dog food aisle deciding

156

what size bag to get. I heard high heels clicking on the tile floor but I didn't pay attention until something hard poked into my ribs. She moved in close beside me and said that she would shoot me if I didn't come along quietly. She took my arm to guide me out of the store and to her car, and I could feel the gun in my ribs the whole time."

"Thank heavens she didn't trip in those high heels and shoot you accidentally," I said. One of the voices in my head said that's exactly what I would have done in her place.

"When we got to the car, she told me to open the door and slide over behind the wheel. Then she handed me a key and told me to drive. We headed to the highway. I tried to drive slowly because I thought I saw you following, Louisa."

I nodded. "I was, but I got stopped by the police for speeding."

"Where did she take you?" Kay asked.

"We were only on the freeway a couple of miles," he said. "She told me to exit at West Elm and we drove to one of the motels at that interchange. She must have checked in earlier. She had a room in the back. We parked in front of it and she slid out of the car first and told me to follow her. And she had a bag from that hardware store next to the grocery. She told me to bring it. It turned out to have a rope in it."

Kay wrinkled her nose. "For some reason, a bag with a rope in it is even more sinister than the gun. What did you talk about in the car?"

"Nothing, really. I said you're making a big

mistake, what's going on, and she just ignored me except for giving directions."

I shivered at the thought of being forced to drive with a silent stranger pointing a gun at me.

"When we got to her room, she kicked the door shut behind her. She told me to sit in the straight chair by the table, and she tied me up. God, I sound like an idiot, letting some woman tie me up without overpowering her and getting away. But she kept the gun on me even when she was dealing with the rope. I figured at that range she couldn't miss, and that being shot would hurt rather a lot."

"What happened after she tied you up?" I asked.

"She asked me where the tape was, and I said I wouldn't tell her. And we repeated that with minor variations for an hour or more. She threatened me with the gun again, but I pointed out if she shot me she'd never learn anything. She opened a bottle of Scotch and sipped it from a glass from the bathroom. Finally she sat down on the bed. She looked exhausted. The only thing she seemed able to focus on was getting hold of the tape."

I suddenly thought of something. "Her car," I said.

"What about it?" he asked.

"When I told Chief Johnson about my car being stolen I forgot to tell him that her car was sitting by the road to your house," I explained. "If it's her own car he can find out who she is from the license plates. It's too old a car to be a rental. I suppose it could have

158

been stolen, if someone else was as stupid as I was and left the keys in the ignition."

"I've done the same thing in my own driveway," Bob consoled. "You couldn't know someone was lurking."

Kay said, "Go call Ed, Louisa, and use the speakerphone so we can hear too." I looked at her blankly. "Press the button that says speaker and when you hear the dial tone, dial," she instructed, and sighed at me.

I went over to the phone on the kitchen counter and did as she instructed. She rattled off the phone number from memory. We listened to the ring, then to Kerry Sue's Maddock's perky voice saying, "Willow Falls Police. How may I help you?"

"This is Louisa McGuire—" I started.

"Hey, Louisa, how you doin'? I don't think I've even talked to you since you moved back to town." There was a little snapping noise. Kerry Sue had always been a gum chewer. "That sure was a shame about your folks. Did your dad suffer much?"

"I don't believe—"

"And your mom, that was really somethin'. She just didn't want to go on without him, did she?"

Out of the corner of my eye I saw Kay and Bob exchange a look, which I interpreted as Kay saying 'I told you so' regarding Kerry Sue's mental prowess.

"Well, no, she—"

"And your husband too. We were sure sorry about your loss." She snapped her gum again.

"Thank you, I—"

"Is it really true that he choked to death in a restaurant while some bimbo was under the table givin' him a blow job?"

I wanted to sink through the floor where I stood. That would put me out of Bob's sight and near the back door, where I could get in Kay's car and either drive away and never come back, or go straight around the block to the police station and kill Kerry Sue. I finally found my voice.

"That's what the papers said, Kerry Sue, but I certainly wasn't there at the time."

"Well, that's a blessing anyway. Say, did you find your car yet?"

"No, I was hoping that you all would be doing that," I said. "May I speak to Chief Johnson, please?"

"Ed? He's not here. He's out driving around somewhere."

"I need to talk to him," I persevered. "Can you have him call me?"

"Yeah, sure, Louisa, you bet. I'll tell him as soon as he comes in."

"Um, this might be important, Kerry Sue. Could you call him now and have him ring me right away?"

"Why? What's up?"

"Well, I—I thought of something that might help him find my car. And I need to tell him soon."

"Your car that got stolen?" More snapping from her gum.

"Right. That car. Please tell him to call me at Kay's number, not mine."

160

"You're at Kay's? I noticed she has the store closed today. How is she?"

Across the room, Kay opened her mouth, miming a scream. I turned my back on her. "She's fine, Kerry Sue. I have to go now. Have Chief Johnson call me soon, okay?"

"Sure, you bet. See you." Her phone clattered down and we heard the dial tone. I couldn't figure out what button to push to disconnect it, so I picked up the receiver and dropped it back in its cradle. When I turned to Kay and Bob, Kay had her head down on her arms and her shoulders were heaving. I wasn't sure if she was laughing or crying. Bob's face was a study.

"Kerry Sue will have Ed call us here," I informed them.

Kay raised her head and I saw tears on her cheeks, but I could tell they were tears of laughter. We looked at each other, then we both shrugged. "She's just as likely to call her Aunt Mildred as Ed," she said.

"I don't think she'll have time," I said. "I'm going over there right now and kill her."

Bob looked alarmed, but Kay said, "Good idea. Certainly no jury of your peers would see it as anything other than justifiable homicide."

"And who would my peers be in this case?"

"Anyone who had ever called the police station when Kerry Sue was on duty."

"True," I said. I made myself look at Bob. "I don't believe I ever mentioned how my husband died."

His expression was carefully neutral. "No reason why you should have. It must have been terrible

161

for you."

"It was," I agreed, "but at least it was worse for him."

21

The phone rang. Since I was still beside it I picked up and said hello. Miraculously, it was Chief Johnson.

"Mrs. McGuire," he said, "I understand you have further information about your car?"

"Not my car, the other one. The Mercedes. The gray one."

"Yes?"

"I forgot to tell you, we saw it. It was parked off the road near the turnoff to Bob's house."

His voice quickened with interest. "When was this?"

"Before we found Bob," I said. "Kay and I saw it there, and that's why we decided to sneak up on his house, so we went through the woods and that's how we found him in the barn."

"So this was, what, two hours ago?"

"I guess it's been that long. At least that. It took us a while to find Bob—"

163

"May I ask why you didn't call me immediately?"

I was stumped for an answer. "I, that is we—um, we were focused on retrieving my car..." I stopped, wondering how 'my cousin didn't want to talk to you' would go over. Maybe saying 'because it would have brought Kerry Sue one conversation closer to her demise' would be better.

"I see. Well, the car isn't there now. I've been driving in that locale myself looking for your car—"

"Thank you. How kind."

"—and there's no gray Mercedes beside that road."

"Oh," I managed. "We were hoping you could find out who the woman is from the license plates."

"What was the number on the plates?" he asked.

I looked across the room at Kay and Bob, who were avidly following my half of this conversation. "Um, hold on," I said, and put my hand over the mouthpiece. "The car's not there anymore," I hissed, "and he wants to know the license number."

Neither of them spoke. Bob finally shook his head.

I took a deep breath and said into the phone, "I'm sorry, none of us got the number."

"Mrs. McGuire, if you should happen to see this gray Mercedes again, it would be extremely helpful if you would get the god damned license plate number," Chief Johnson said evenly.

"Yes," I told him. "I will. Goodbye." I could hear

his voice still squawking from the receiver as I hung up.

"He's pissed at us, isn't he?" my cousin asked, and I nodded. She shrugged and got up from the table, going to the freezer for more ice. "Well, at least one thing is still normal. Who needs more tea?"

"I need something, though I'm not sure tea is strong enough," I said. "Arsenic maybe."

"My tea is strong enough," Kay assured me. "Save the arsenic for Kerry Sue."

Bob took my glass and his own to the kitchen and held them out for cubes. He set the glasses on the counter and Kay poured more tea from the pitcher. Bob leaned a hip against the counter.

"I have to confess that after listening to Kerry Sue, I no longer know what we were talking about," he said.

"The woman in red," Kay said instantly. "But I want to go back to something else. Bob, you said the stepfather didn't know that Ian was seeing you?"

"I don't think he did," Bob agreed.

Kay went on, "So how did he know about the tape or that you were any kind of threat? You really think the police detective told him?"

"I know it sounds crazy, but he's the only person I told about the tape. Of course, my other patients know I tape all my sessions but—"

"So is that why you didn't want to talk to Ed in the car?" I asked. "Because you don't trust the cops?"

Bob nodded. "I don't know who to trust, other than you. Probably the Willow Falls police are safe,

165

but the High Cross detective could have told Ian's stepfather I had an incriminating video."

"What does Ian's stepfather look like? And what the heck is his name? We keep calling him the stepfather," I said.

"His name is Carl Walsh, and he's a big guy, over six feet and broad. Not fat, just wide. Football player type. You can imagine him in a high school game creaming smaller guys and walking off smiling."

"He sounds like the man who was searching my car," I said. "So that's why Jack reacted the way he did. He was really terrified when he saw who it was. And we were all scared when Walsh almost caught us in the barn."

"What?" Bob stared at me. "What do you mean, he almost caught you in the barn?"

"I ran away through the woods when I saw him searching my car. I was in the upper part of the barn, the same place we discovered you, catching my breath. I heard him go into the lower part. Then he went around and came in the upper door but I was hiding behind those same hay bales where you were sleeping."

He shook his head at me. "My god, Louisa. If he had found you..." He swallowed. "How did you get away?"

"A mouse ran by him and I guess he thought it wouldn't be there if we were around. Then a dog barked outside. He took off." It sounded frighteningly flimsy to my ears. I told myself to go back to the barn soon and leave a wheel of brie for that mouse.

Silence fell around the table. Kay finally spoke.

"You know what I'd like to do next," she said, turning to Bob. "I want to see the tape of Ian's session with you. Where is it?"

Bob made a face. "Well, the original is gone, it was stolen from my safety deposit box, which is what made me leave town."

Kay and I both stared at him. "Stolen from your safety deposit box!" Kay finally sputtered. "How the hell did they manage that?"

"Walsh, Ian's stepfather, runs the bank. He owns it. It was started by his wife's family several generations ago and he inherited it when she died."

We digested the implications of that, then I said, "That was the original. How about this copy? Did you give that one to the police?"

He shook his head. "I made one copy, figured I'd give it to the cops. But the detective was so awful I just kept it in my pocket. After I found Jack, I stashed it in his dog food bin. A day or so later I went to the bank to get the original so I could make a second back up copy, and that's when I discovered it was missing."

"Did you tell them at the bank it was gone from your box?" Kay asked.

"No. It was just too weird. And that was about the time I remembered Ian saying his stepfather ran a bank. I had no idea it was my bank. I mean, how many people know who runs their bank?"

"Well, I do, but that's because I've known Harold since he was a pup," Kay said.

"What did you do?" I asked.

167

"I called my lawyer, who told me to get out of town and hide."

"Why Willow Falls?" Kay asked.

"My lawyer's brother owns the stone house and she asked him to let me use it. Which now seems to have left too direct a trail. I grabbed a few necessities and Jack and the copy of the tape and came to Willow Falls."

Kay stood up. "Let's go get it. Is it still in the dog food?"

Bob shook his head. "I was afraid they'd find me sooner or later, so I hid it somewhere else."

"Where?" she demanded.

"Do you remember the day Louisa and I met, when we stopped in your store and said hello?"

"Sure, I called your dog a jack rabbit and we talked about bad furniture. It was just a couple of weeks ago."

"I had the tape with me in my backpack that day. In fact, that's why I was walking around. I was looking for someplace to hide the tape, someplace that would be so unconnected to me that Walsh wouldn't find it, even if he located me."

"So where is it?" Kay asked.

"When Louisa and I met and we walked down Maple Street it occurred to me that perhaps I could hide it in one of the shops. The two of you left the room to get something, and I hid the tape in your store."

Kay jumped up and headed for the stairs. "Let's go."

22

We clattered down into Kay's combination office and workroom. The unlit store was still and dim. The light she switched on sliced into the dark, brightening her sales desk. Bob strode into the store and looked around as Kay turned on more lights. He frowned and moved to the arched doorway into the larger sales room.

"Have you moved things around?" he turned to ask Kay. She shrugged, walking toward him. I was a couple of paces behind her.

"I'm always moving things around."

"Where do you think she got those biceps?" I added. She threw me a look over her shoulder.

"Things sell and move out, and we rearrange to highlight other pieces. What are you looking for?"

"That big awful whatever it was," Bob said, waving his arms to indicate size and awfulness.

"Not the Albatross—that ridiculous armoire-sideboard-wine cooler-secretary thing?" she said, stopping in her tracks. I walked into her back and bounced off.

"That's the one," he replied. Kay shook her head.

"I sold it," she said.

His eyes widened. "But you said it was so awful no one would ever buy it. You were going to have to be buried in it."

"Well, yeah, but that was before I knew of any people as tasteless as the owners of a restaurant in High Cross that Ambrose is decorating. He took them a picture of it and they loved it. He picked it up this morning in fact."

"That's where you hid the tape?" I broke in. "In the Albatross?"

Bob nodded. "You and Kay left me alone, and I saw a roll of mailing tape on the counter. I used it to attach the video onto the back of a drawer."

Kay and I stared as Bob's expression turned sheepish. "It seemed like a good idea at the time. I thought I'd seen a car like Walsh's while Louisa and I were at the Bluebird and I had the tape in my backpack. I didn't want him to catch me with it."

"Geez," Kay said. We looked at each other for a couple of heartbeats. She gave a broad shrug. "Well, I did say that no one was ever going to buy it. I'll go call Ambrose. Maybe he can do something about getting it back." She hurried toward her office and the phone.

A knock on the front door of the store made my heart begin to clamor. "Now what?" Kay exclaimed.

The door knob rattled, followed by more knocking, louder this time.

"Do you want me to see who it is?" I called.

"No, I'll get it. I'm halfway there already." I heard Kay's footsteps cross to the door and the sound of the locks being opened. The pulled-down shade clattered like dry bones as she jerked the door open. Bob and I remained where we were, beside a big cherry armoire that blocked our view of the front door. "Yes, what is it?" she said in a decidedly uncordial voice. Not the way she usually speaks to a potential customer.

"Oh, good, you are here," came a loud voice. A woman's voice.

Doris's voice.

I locked eyes with Bob. We didn't move.

The loud Doris voice continued. "I was here a couple of weeks ago and saw something that I've decided I want to buy—"

"I sold it," Kay snapped out. The bell on the door jangled a little, as though Kay had tried to close the door and been stopped.

Doris said, "I haven't even told you what it was. How the hell would you know if you'd sold it?"

Only someone who knew Kay as well as I do would have heard the minute pause before she said, "I remember what you were looking at. It's been sold."

Doris could have been cross examining a hostile witness. "Oh yes? And just what do you remember me looking at two weeks ago, when you barely noticed my presence in this store?"

And where were you on the night of last January twenty-third at 9:42 p.m. when the crime was taking place? I added mentally.

"You strolled through my store in a counter clockwise circle, pausing before any piece of furniture made of pine. You picked up a silver cocktail shaker and put it down in a different place, and you handled a couple of porcelain figurines. But I imagine the piece you're talking about is the painted pine handkerchief box that you looked at for several minutes, set down, and returned to twice before you left the store. I sold it to the next person who walked in, a widow from Milwaukee who remembered her mother having one like it in Pennsylvania. The piece is gone. Rare items like that do not wait for your convenience. Now, my store is closed for the day. Goodbye." I heard the thump of the door closing, the click of the locks being set again.

Bob looked at me in astonishment. "Good lord, your cousin is amazing," he managed, as Kay's footsteps came back toward us.

I could have told him that.

"Did you hear that?" Kay demanded as she came back into our view. "Doesn't that woman ever go home? She lives in Seattle, for goodness' sake! What the hell is she doing in my store all the time?"

"She has clients all over," I told her. "She's famous for her knowledge of import and export law. She's always jetting somewhere. Roger used to complain about it. I think he was jealous."

"Well, let her jet somewhere else," Kay said crossly. "Now, what was I doing when we were so rudely interrupted? Oh, I know. I was about to call Ambrose." She turned again to go to the phone.

The next thing I knew I had burst out laughing. I felt decidedly out of control. They stared at me. I flapped a hand at them. When I could catch my breath enough to speak I said, "Sorry, sorry, it's just...the last twenty four hours have been so ridiculous. All of us moving around in our own little circles, me lost in the woods and hiding in the barn and trudging through suburbia. Bob tied to a chair being grilled by a beautiful blonde and sneaking away. Ambrose in here carting away the Albatross. What's his name looking for the tape which is now in a restaurant somewhere in High Cross. The way things are going we'll probably learn that the restaurant is next door to the bank they stole the original tape from. And now Doris has circled her way back here to buy a wooden box that you sold two weeks ago..." I faltered at Kay's expression.

She shook her head. "If I had time I'd slap you out of this hysteria," she sniffed. "You ought to know our inventory better than that. The box hasn't been sold, it's sitting about three feet away from you on that dresser. I told you I don't take money with cooties on it." She marched back to her office. I looked at the dresser, and saw the box. My laughing jag was over. I hiccupped.

Bob took my hand between both of his. "Would she really slap you?" His look of concern made my breath catch in my throat.

I managed a shrug. "Probably not unless she thought I was really out of control. I'm okay now. You were right earlier when you said things like this don't happen to people like us."

"I don't know what I'd have done if you hadn't found me in the barn," Bob said, shaking his head. "Gone on the run again, maybe. Or gone blundering back into that woman's hands."

"Well, we can't have her catching you again," I said. "You should have called me as soon as you got loose."

"Call me old fashioned," he smiled, "but I never got into the habit of calling a lady at three a.m. And I do not want you involved in this thing. I can't believe how I've put you in danger. If Walsh had found you in the barn, I don't think he'd have been as polite as my kidnapper was."

I was silent as I imagined some distinctly unpleasant scenarios. I remembered another detail we had not yet covered. "I need to know something else," I told him.

"Anything."

"Who is Trixie?"

Kay bustled back into the room. "Ambrose is coming, but it's going to take him a while to get here," she announced. I saw one of her eyebrows go up as she noted Bob holding my hand.

"Oh, good," Bob said, glancing over at her. Then he turned back to me. "Trixie? I don't think I know anyone with that name."

"I found a book of matches on your kitchen table. 'Trixie' and a phone number were written inside."

"On my kitchen table?" His brow puckered. He

shook his head. "I have absolutely no idea. I rarely use matches, and I don't know any Trixie."

"Oh. Okay," I said, taking my hand from his.

While we were waiting for Ambrose, Bob said he'd like to take a shower. I made him hand out his clothes so that we could give them a quick wash and dry. "You'll find new toothbrushes and disposable razors in the medicine chest," I told him through the door. I heard him thank me as the shower started.

Kay put laundry soap in the washer and I dumped in Bob's clothes. As she fiddled with the dials I turned to her. "Kay, I want to ask you about something."

"Yeah?"

"I should have asked a long time ago, and I'm sorry I've been so self-centered that I didn't do it before now." I spun the dial on the washer and pushed it in to start the wash cycle.

She looked surprised and a little wary. "Yeah? What?"

"What happened with you and Ed?"

"What do you mean, what happened? We went out for a while and then we stopped."

I know Kay as well as she knows me, and I knew that stonewalling tone of voice. "Uh-uh. Nope. There's more to it than that. I remember some of your phone calls to me in Seattle when the two of you were first going out. You sounded like a teenager. You were having a really great time together. But about the time my life got complicated—"

"That's one way to put it," she inserted.

"When my life got complicated you stopped talking about yours. When I moved back to Willow Falls, no Ed to be seen, and any time his name comes up you practically spit. Of course now that I've met him, the question is what you ever saw in him in the first place—"

"I should think that at least would be perfectly obvious!"

"What?"

"Well, Louisa, you've seen him. You have to admit he's pretty darned gorgeous."

"Oh. Oh yeah, that," I said. An amazed voice in my head said, oh my god, she is still in love with this guy. Where I saw slightly tubby middle aged cop, she saw Adonis.

"Okay, looks aside," I tried tactfully, "he *is* pretty maddening—"

"But you've only met him once," she leapt to his defense. How could she not see what she still felt for him? "He takes his job seriously, and he's good at it. You should see all the letters of commendation he's gotten, and he solved some very complicated cases when he was with the state police."

"Well, if you say so. I happen to think a *really* good cop would never call you 'lady' in that sarcastic tone of voice, but you know him better. But how did you go from being a teenager in love to so pissed you can't talk to him on the phone for two minutes?"

Her eyes dropped. She turned and closed the top of the detergent box and put it back on its shelf,

176

fiddling to get it perfectly aligned. Then she wiped a few grains of detergent off the lid of the washer. At last she turned back and said, "I just hate to talk about it. It sounds so stupid. We broke up over a parking ticket."

"A parking ticket?"

"Well, you know how crowded Maple Street has gotten, right? Some days you can't find a parking place for blocks, and all of us who have businesses here depend on people being able to get to our stores. Most of the people who work in the area drive as well. We've had a lot of hassle about employees parking their cars on the street. And the police station and city hall are only a couple of blocks away, and the people who work there need to park too."

I nodded. Even in the daze in which I had co-cooned myself for the past six months, I was aware of the parking problem. The city council made a couple of vacant lots into parking areas and put time limits on the street parking places a few months ago, and the police were quick to write tickets if you overstayed your two-hour welcome.

"So about the time everyone was so worked up about parking and that's all we talked about at city council meetings, I noticed that Ed and the other cops parked their cruisers in the two hour spaces and sometimes left them half the day. They were out giving other people tickets for staying too long, but they weren't willing to walk two blocks from the station or move their own cars. So I brought it up at a council meeting."

"Did you talk to Ed about it before you brought it up at the council?"

She looked abashed. "Well, no. I was already kind of mad at him because of his mother and his daughter."

I held up a hand to stop her. "Wait. Wait. I know you're about to digress and I will never find out what happened at the council meeting. Keep going and we will come back for the mother and daughter."

She laughed and leaned her hip on the now-vibrating washer. "I see you still have your meeting facilitation skills intact," she teased. "Okay, we'll take his mother and daughter under advisement."

"Good."

"I happened to mention at a council meeting that I thought it was unfair for the cops to be able to park their cars on the street all day while they gave tickets to other people for the same thing."

"I'm just curious, did you casually mention it or did you raise a stink?"

"Okay, okay, maybe a little bitty stink. I wasn't ranting and raving and waving my arms or anything. But it ended up with the council instructing Ed to tell his deputies they had to follow the rules too, and he was pretty peeved. And you're right, he was mostly mad about me blindsiding him with it."

"Yeah, I imagine so."

She sighed. "I don't know why I was so stupid. Of course I should have talked to him about it first, but I just blurted it out in public."

"We all do stuff like that though. My mouth has

gotten me in trouble plenty of times."

A twinkle gleamed into her eye. "We'll take that under advisement too. I'm going to want to hear about this. Anyway, about a week later, I had to run a quick errand. I started out but realized I'd forgotten to grab the mail and I was going near the post office. So I circled the block and saw a parking place right in front of my door. I ran inside for the mail, and the phone rang, and one thing led to another, and before I knew it a couple of hours had passed. I suddenly remembered my car was parked on the street instead of behind the building. So I went out to move it, and there was Ed writing a parking ticket."

"Uh-oh."

"Right. I told him I was moving my car and it could only been a hair over the two hours, but he kept writing that damned ticket and saying something about what's good for the gander ought to be good enough for the goose."

"He didn't!"

"I wanted to smack him but he would have arrested me for attacking a police officer in the execution of his duty. So I grabbed the ticket and tore it into little bitty pieces and threw them at him and got in my car and drove it around back and parked it and practically busted the door slamming it when I got out. I stomped around kicking the walls for a few minutes until I was a little calmer. When I went back in the store, I found a new parking ticket lying on the counter, plus another ticket for littering. Which I have not paid, either of them. And we've barely spoken to each

179

other since."

"Wow," I breathed. "I haven't given him enough credit for bravery."

"Damn straight. He's lucky he's still walking around. He could have ended up like that TV cop in the wheelchair."

"When did all this happen?"

"Oh, about two seconds before Roger died, which is why you never heard about it. Didn't seem right to be talking about parking tickets just then."

I reached over and gave her a hug. The spinning washer vibrated us both. "I should have had the brains to ask, but as you know I haven't been able to find my head with both hands for months. But I am better, mostly thanks to you."

She shook her head. "I didn't do anything that any upstanding and loyal cousin wouldn't have done. I think Bob has made all the difference."

"There you go again, changing the subject."

"I'd say he *is* the subject, or at least his duds are. Looks like they're ready to put into the dryer."

I opened the dryer door and she threw the clothes in. As I set the timer I said, "Okay, so now to the tabled part of the agenda. What's the deal with Ed's mother and daughter?"

"I think they really started all the trouble between us. We were getting along okay. Not that we didn't argue about stuff, because he's really pigheaded sometimes, but that was okay. It wasn't serious fighting, just some bickering."

"Fun stuff," I suggested.

She grinned. "Yeah, actually it was." Then her expression turned serious. "You know his wife had died—"

"Cancer, I think you said?"

"Yeah, she had breast cancer. He still worked for the state police then, but after she died he took an early retirement. But that made him crazy with nothing to do so he came to Willow Falls. His mother moved in with him and his daughter Faith to keep house and take care of them. That's her story, anyway. I think she just loves to tell people what to do. I don't know how he stands her. Faith is a great kid though."

"But what did they have to do with you and Ed?"

"Well, you can't get away from family, can you? Mrs. Johnson decided as soon as she met me that she hated me, so she was constantly pushing at Ed to break up with me. And Faith and I really hit it off, and she was pushing her dad to marry me. So with one of them pushing in one direction and the other in the other—"

"I bet he was wishing he'd never heard of you."

"Right. And the thing with the parking just sent it right over the edge."

"What about you, what do you want? Wouldn't you like to try again?"

"Hell, no," she said robustly. "My life is just fine the way it is. At least it will be as soon as we get hold of that tape of Bob's and get this murderer taken care of. Come on, let's go call Trixie's number again, and tell Bob his clothes are drying."

23

A heavenly smell preceded Ambrose up the stairs from the shop. He entered the apartment bearing gifts: two large, fragrant pizza boxes. "Hello, Louisa, Bob. I picked up something to nosh on. Kay and I both think better with pizza in front of us," he explained.

She took the boxes and set them on the dining table, saying, "Doesn't everyone? Though it does seem like we've had a meal every twenty minutes today."

Ambrose shrugged off his tweed sport coat and adjusted the cuffs of his periwinkle silk shirt. "God, Kay, this pizza habit goes back to that very first one we made all those years ago, when we were designing the costumes for the school play."

I went to the kitchen for knives and forks while Bob got beers and soft drinks out of the refrigerator. Kay handed out napkins from the basket that holds her collection of those-that-don't-matter-if-you-get-pizza-sauce-all-over-them.

"I can barely remember that long ago," she said, shaking her head. "Chef Boyardee pizza in a box—a little packet of dough mix, and a little can of sauce, and a little packet of desiccated cheese. I was in the eighth grade and you were a mighty sophomore, and I wasn't sure I'd like this pizza stuff but you were so incredibly sophisticated that I had to act like I did no matter what it tasted like. Was that your first pizza too? I never knew that."

We settled with the dogs at our feet. Their interested faces clearly expressed their hope that pizza bones would fall on the floor. The bagels we'd consumed earlier had no effect on our willingness to attack the contents of the boxes. Ambrose spread his napkin on his lap and picked up his knife and fork. As he cut into his slice of pizza, he said, "Oh, yes, that was me at the age of fifteen, the complete cosmopolitan." He looked around the table at each of us. "I understand that I carried away the Albatross at just the wrong moment, but that's about all I do understand." He conveyed a neat bite of pizza to his mouth and chewed.

Kay paused in her reach for a pizza slice and looked at Bob and me. "Permission to speak freely? I can vouch for Ambrose's trustworthiness."

"Of course," I said, and Bob nodded. Kay turned to Ambrose.

"Bob is a hypnotherapist. He had a copy of a video of a session with a client who, while under hypnosis, remembered seeing his stepfather in the house on the night that his mother died."

"That sounds fraught with peril," Ambrose said. Kay nodded.

"Her death was ruled a suicide because Carl Walsh, the stepfather, had an alibi for being elsewhere, and Ian had blanked out the memory of seeing him in the house. We think that Ian confronted his stepfather with his recovered memory, because Ian died the same way his mother had, an apparent suicide."

Ambrose had cut another bite, and hastily swallowed it so he could ask, "I take it, Bob, that you hid this tape in the ungainly piece of furniture I hauled out of here this morning?"

Bob nodded. "Except that the tape in the Albatross is a copy of the original. I put the original in my safety deposit box in my bank in High Cross. What I didn't know at the time was that Walsh owns that bank—he inherited it from Ian's mother. I don't know how he got into my box, but that's where I kept the original tape."

"My goodness," Ambrose paused in cutting another bite, "is nothing sacred?"

I had just taken a big bite of pizza, and strings of cheese were festooned from my lips back to the slice. I was trying to separate myself from the cheese when Ambrose's mild rhetorical question struck me as wildly funny under the circumstances and I snorted with laughter. This had the effect of drawing all eyes to me. I chewed hastily. "Sorry, don't mind me."

Kay frowned and went on. "It's possible that a police detective tipped Carl off to the existence of the

184

tape. Bob tried to tell him about his suspicions, but the detective brushed him off. But he was the only person Bob told about the tape."

"Suggestive."

"When the tape disappeared, Bob figured if this guy had killed twice, it wouldn't be safe to hang around and wait for him to do it again. So he came to Willow Falls to hide while he figures out what to do."

"So, is the possible untrustworthiness of the police the reason we are having this cozy discussion of murder without the help of Ed or any of his minions?" Ambrose asked.

"Right," said Kay. "I don't *think* Ed would spill the beans. But he is still mad at me, and now he's peeved at Louisa for not getting the license number of Bob's kidnapper."

Ambrose's eyes widened. "Kidnapper!"

"Last night Bob was kidnapped when he went into the Food Right near his house," I explained.

"By the bad guy? My god, Bob, how did you get away?" He sat up straighter in his chair.

Bob shook his head. Kay said, "No, he was taken at gunpoint by a woman. We don't know who she is but we think she must be working with Walsh. Bob was able to hypnotize her into a deep sleep and get away, and Louisa and I found him in an old barn near his house when we were going to get Louisa's car."

"Ah, Louisa's car." Ambrose looked at me. "I *was* a trifle surprised to see you arrive here this morning with the two dogs in a taxi. What happened to your car?"

Why do people always ask you a question just as you've taken a bite of food? I've long been convinced that waiters are trained to do it—they sweep by and ask "Is everything all right?" just as you've inserted your fork into your mouth, so you can only mumble, and they sweep away again, leaving you no chance to say anything, and your only opportunity to ask for a clean knife or another napkin is gone. This didn't seem like the time to ask Ambrose if he had ever worked as a waiter. I held up my hand to indicate I needed a moment, and Kay jumped in.

"Louisa was waiting in Bob's car last night when he went into the grocery store. She saw him come out and drive away in the other woman's car. She went to Bob's house this morning to see if he was back, and while she was there she saw a strange man searching her car."

"Which, if I'm remembering correctly, looks exactly like Bob's car," Ambrose said.

"Right. We assume he thought he was searching Bob's, but his is still parked in Louisa's garage. When Louisa saw the guy at her car, she ran out the back door with the dogs and got lost in the woods and eventually got to a phone and called a cab and came here, which is when you saw her."

She made me sound like an idiot, and I knew I'd certainly looked like one when I arrived at her store. "It wasn't just the woods," I said, "it was him searching in the barn while we were hiding behind the hay bales—"

Bob looked upset. "I still can't believe he came

so close to finding you in the barn."

"—and that neighborhood with all those stupid curving streets that look alike. I thought we'd never find our way out. It was almost worse than being in the woods."

Ambrose peered at me with real sympathy. "That must have been frightening, Louisa, though I don't think either of these dogs would let anyone harm you." He added judiciously, "And I've been lost in places like that neighborhood myself. Believe me, you were lucky to escape merely damp and with a cab bill."

"Uh, thanks," was all I could come up with. The image of Ambrose lost in a suburban housing tract beggared the imagination.

Kay swept on. "When we got to Bob's house we were just in time to see the woman in red—"

"Woman in red?" Ambrose repeated.

"She was wearing a red suit when she marched me out of the grocery store," Bob explained.

"Only when we saw her again she'd changed clothes and had on a red plaid shirt," I added.

Ambrose nodded. "I see. Go on, please."

"Thank you. I will." Kay glared at Bob and me. I forbore to point out that it was Ambrose who had interrupted her. "We arrived just in time to see this woman drive off in Louisa's car. I called Ed, I mean the police, but we haven't heard anything about the car yet. We came back here and made Bob tell us what's going on."

"We wanted to watch the tape of Ian's hypnosis session," I added.

"Which I hid in Kay's store," said Bob. "I was afraid that Carl would catch up with me sooner or later. There would be no reason for him to look here for the tape."

"And when we went downstairs to get it, we learned he'd hidden it in the Albatross, which you picked up this morning," Kay said. "So now we need to get the tape back. And we're waiting to hear from the police about Louisa's car, and we're waiting for another shoe to drop. We don't know when or where Carl or the woman in red will show up."

"And there's Trixie," I added.

"Who's Trixie?" Ambrose asked. "Is someone really named Trixie?"

"We don't know if that's her real name. I found a matchbook from a local bar on Bob's kitchen table this morning, with the name Trixie and a phone number written inside."

"I swear I've never seen it before," Bob said. "I have no idea how it came to be in my house."

"And every time we call the number, the line is busy," Kay finished.

Ambrose shook his head and took another bite of pizza. He chewed thoughtfully, then swallowed and said, "The searching of the car—don't you think it's interesting that they were there at different times? It seems to me if they were working together they'd be searching it together."

"But the woman in red probably hadn't woken up yet, it was quite early," I said.

"And Carl must have thought she had me tied

188

up in her hotel room while he was searching the car," Bob pointed out.

"Yes, and why was he searching a perfectly innocent car when he could have been in the hotel room interrogating you, or worse?" Ambrose frowned and shook his head. "It would have been much more intimidating for the two of them to be working you over rather than just her. Did she talk to him on the phone?"

Now it was Bob's turn to shake his head. "No. No calls in or out. I don't think she even looked at the telephone."

"I have to wonder if they aren't working at cross purposes. My guess is that she took Louisa's car to give herself time to search it thoroughly. You had escaped and could show up at any time."

Bob said, "That's possible."

"Are your two cars really so identical?" Ambrose asked.

"I can't tell them apart," I told him, "unless I look to see what stuff is left inside. About the only thing that's not the same is their locks. And the license plates."

"And I suppose the registration papers are different," Ambrose remarked.

"Oh, god, that's right," Kay groaned. She shoved her plate away from her. "Louisa, all they have to do is read the papers in your glovebox to know where you live."

Bob looked pale. "Oh god, that's right."

"By now they've probably been to your house,"

Kay continued, "and found Bob's car in your garage. It isn't safe, either or both of them could be there."

An electrical impulse zapped its way down my back and left me chilled. I leaned forward in my chair. "Um, Kay, that's not all that was in my glove box."

"What? What else?" she demanded.

"Do you remember those business cards you gave me when I started working for you, with the name of your store and my name on them?"

She paled a little. "They were there too?"

I nodded. "I keep a supply in the car in case I'm out and need one for some reason. And that means—"

"And that means they know about this place," Bob said. He stood up abruptly. "My god, what have I done to you all? Louisa has to get to someplace safe. Kay, you too. You're both in danger." Jack went to Bob and leaned on him.

"I agree that getting to a safe place while I fetch the tape from that benighted restaurant in High Cross is a good idea," Ambrose said. "Though I think the person most in danger is you, Bob."

Bob started to speak, but Ambrose held up a hand. He went on, "Two people are intent on finding you. The fact that Louisa had your car would suggest that they might look upon her with a certain disfavor too. The business cards make it likely they'll come here looking for you, but they won't know Kay is Louisa's cousin or be certain that she knows anything. But best to be safe.

"Here's my suggestion. I have a cabin in the woods out near Parson's Lake, a little getaway place I inherited from my uncle. It's about thirty-five miles north of here. You can all go there tonight, and in the morning I will get the tape and bring it to you at the cabin. The Albatross is either still on the truck or in the delivery company's warehouse. I'll make some phone calls tonight but I doubt if I can get at it until tomorrow."

"I can't go," Kay stated flatly. We all looked at her. "Hey, I have a store to run. I can't keep chasing customers out of here, though in Doris's case I would have done it even if I had been open."

"I beg your pardon?" Ambrose was clearly at sea over this remark.

"Oh, that awful Doris woman who worked with Louisa's husband showed up at my door earlier wanting to buy something. We had just discovered that the tape was carried off in the Albatross and I didn't want to mess with her, so I wouldn't let her in."

"I don't imagine she knows you're my cousin," I inserted. "We should tell her so she'll stop coming around."

"What makes you think that would stop her?" Kay wanted to know. "I'm sure she would relish further opportunities to be rude to you."

"True," I had to agree.

"Anyway, Ambrose may be my favorite customer but he's not my only one. I've arranged for some pieces to be picked up early tomorrow, and I need to be here."

"But, Kay—" I started. She interrupted.

"I closed today and that was no problem, but I

191

have appointments tomorrow and I won't stay in business if I'm not here when I've said I would be."

"But, Kay—" I tried again.

"Ambrose is right, Louisa, just because you work for me doesn't mean I would necessarily know anything about Bob. I could say you don't work here anymore. I could blacken your name." She got a zealous light in her eye and started looking eager. "If someone does show up asking about Bob, I'll send them off in the wrong direction. I can say that I fired you and the two of you ran off together. Oh, I know, I can say you ran off together and that's *why* I fired you—"

"Kay, don't do us any favors," I warned.

Bob sat down at the table again and looked earnestly into Kay's eyes. "Kay, you should come with us. Call your customer and put them off. Or come back early in the morning. I can't leave you here to face Carl Walsh by yourself. You've never even seen him. He could pretend to be a customer and come in and do something awful."

"Bob, you are very sweet, but my mind is made up. I have a business to run. I'll bar the doors and arm myself with a butcher knife and a cell phone. Remember, you're the one they're after."

I could have told him to save his breath. I'd seen that expression on her face too many times to imagine she would agree. Short of kidnapping her ourselves, Kay was going to stay in Willow Falls and we were going to Ambrose's cabin.

Kay always gets her own way.

24

Bob turned off the engine of Kay's car and we sat in silence, looking at the cabin in the headlights.

"Maybe we can spend the night in the car," I said.

"Yeah, maybe."

The place was a wreck. I couldn't understand why Ambrose had sent us here. A sagging porch stretched across the front of a small, weathered building. If any paint had ever graced the wooden walls, it had long since silvered away. The roof was littered with pine needles and leaves, and green things were growing along the edges. Shutters over the windows gave the cabin a lost, blind air.

"We're here. We might as well get out," Bob said halfheartedly.

"This can't be the right place," I said. "Are you sure it's safe? It looks like it will keel over if I lean against a wall."

"We followed the directions exactly. It's not like we had a lot of roads to choose from," he pointed out.

"I cannot believe Ambrose ever spent one second of his life here."

"I know, but this has to be it. There must be more to Ambrose than meets the eye."

"Well, that's true," I admitted. I suddenly remembered a certain period in high school when jocks kept losing their clothes while they were in football practice. They would arrive naked and dripping from the showers to find nothing in their lockers but a note typed on ordinary notebook paper that said, *You boys be nice.* Oddly enough the only victims were the boys who ganged up on other kids and made their lives a misery because they were not overdeveloped, physically adept and ordained to play high school sports. It didn't happen every day, just often enough to keep them all edgy. No one ever found out who was doing it, though I always had my suspicions, but the clothes turned up at the local Goodwill store at Christmastime.

Emily Ann reached over the back of the seat and poked my neck with her cold nose. "Okay, Emily Ann, okay, we'll get out," I told her, and unclipped my seatbelt.

The two stairs to the porch creaked ominously as I trod on them, and the porch itself had a definite sway. Bob fished the key Ambrose had given him out of his pocket, and fitted it into the lock in the door. After only a minor struggle it turned, proving we had the right place. Damn.

Bob took a deep breath. "Louisa, I am very sorry about all this." He looked as tired as I felt. It had been a long day.

My throat tightened. I managed to croak, "You haven't done anything to be sorry for. Open the door."

He turned the knob and shoved. I expected creaking hinges and festoons of cobwebs to sweep across my face, but the door swung open silently. Bob groped around for the light switch, and flipped it on. We stepped inside and halted.

My first impression was that the room consisted entirely of an enormous bed—it was so magnificent that it was all I could see. Four tall, slender posters were hung with linen draperies, and a matching spread with exquisite cutwork embroidery covered the mattress, which was so high off the floor that a set of steps was necessary to enable one to retire. I felt my cheeks pinken until I noticed the rest of the furniture between me and that bed in the cabin's single room. A pair of overstuffed chairs and a loveseat, upholstered in dark brown linen, flanked a stone fireplace with logs laid ready to light on its hearth. A low round table filled the space between the seating pieces, and side tables held tall lamps with painted glass bases and linen covered shades. A small kitchen area was to the left, round dining table and four chairs at one end.

I knew from Kay that Ambrose was considered an excellent decorator and had the clients to prove it. Now I saw for myself how this room reached out and wrapped itself around you in a warm welcome.

We took a couple more steps into the room and looked at each other. "Wow," Bob remarked, and I nodded.

"A little getaway cabin in the woods," I said. "I wonder if I could get him to work on my house."

"This is great."

"I'm sure I could never afford him. Maybe he gives discounts to people he's known a long time. I could get Kay to ask."

Resting on the mantel was a large painting of a windswept plain with a single farmhouse in the near distance. An Amish quilt of the center diamond pattern was hung on the wall between the two front windows, its intricate quilting thrown into relief by the light. While Bob opened the shutters to let in some air, I peered closely at the quilt, trying to count the incredibly tiny stitches that made up the feathered rope design.

Jack busied himself checking out the room, sniffing around in a thoughtful manner. Emily Ann went straight to one of the big chairs, climbed up and settled down with her chin resting on the arm.

A closed door flanked each side of the bed. After freeing the windows, Bob walked over and opened the one nearer the fireplace: a large closet, with room for hanging clothes on one side and shelves on the other, holding a variety of household items: blankets, linens, cleaning supplies, light bulbs. I went around the bed and tried the other door. When I switched on the light I saw this was the bathroom—or rather Bathroom.

This must have been added some years after

the cabin was built, which most likely had an out-house in its early days. The room was the shape of a traditional lean-to addition, but much taller, and the high ceiling allowed for a row of clerestory windows above the roofline of the cabin itself. The toilet was in an alcove to my left, with a door leading to the outdoors beside it. An enormous old fashioned claw-footed tub on my right had a shower suspended over it. In front of me was a wall of glass that during the day would doubtless lend the impression one was bathing in the woods.

Overhead was a crystal chandelier, tinkling like a glass of iced tea in the faint breeze from the still-open front door. Its myriad of sparkling drops gleamed in the light of five clear bulbs, throwing shards of brightness around the room. Bob came up behind me and looked in, his gaze caught by the chandelier.

"Waterford," I remarked. He looked startled.

"What?"

"It's a Waterford chandelier," I explained.

He looked at the chandelier. "Wow, you're good. How many people could tell that by one look?"

"Probably a lot, but don't be too impressed. Kay sold it to Ambrose just after I moved back to Willow Falls. I never knew what he did with it, though."

His smile turned into a laugh. "Louisa, I love your honesty."

My smile faded, and he quickly sobered. "What?" he asked. "What is it?"

I shook my head once. "There's so much you don't know about me—"

197

One arm came around my shoulders in a quick hug, then he gave me a little shake. "Louisa," he said sternly, "we've only known each other for a couple of weeks. Of course there's a lot I don't know about you."

"And what you do know is awful."

"What are you talking about? I don't know anything that's awful about you."

I felt the bridge of my nose prickle with tears that wanted to be shed. "The idiotic way my husband died—"

"But that wasn't *you*, that was his idiocy. And while I'd like to claim you know everything about me since I narrated what felt like my whole life story this afternoon, probably still one or two events remain that you haven't heard about. I admit I can't think of anything quite so spectacular as what Kerry Sue described, but some of mine are fairly idiotic.

"Now, come on. Let's close that front door that should have shrieked like a banshee when we opened it but didn't. I'll make you some of my famous cocoa if we can find anything to make it with, or tea if not. And we'll sit down and relax for the first time in, what is it, twenty-four hours? A week and a half? When did I walk into that grocery store anyway?"

He took my hand, led me back into the other room and over to the love seat. Gently he pushed me down onto it; it felt good to settle into the cushions. Jack immediately jumped up beside me. "Good boy," Bob told him, "you keep Louisa company for me." He gave Emily Ann's head a quick stroke as he passed her. He closed the front door and moved over to the kitchen area.

This was tiny, with a small stove and refrigerator, a microwave, some open shelves on the wall. Dark brown tiles topped the counters, and under the window a single porcelain sink gleamed. I watched over the back of the love seat as Bob busied himself opening all the cabinets, the refrigerator and freezer. Mother Hubbard would have felt right at home—nothing to make cocoa, no tea, no coffee. However, a full bar was set up in an old dry sink under a window looking out to the side yard. Bob opened a bottle of pinot noir and poured generous amounts into two glasses.

"I wonder if I should drive back to that little town we passed," he remarked as he set the glasses on the table in front of the couch. "I don't know about you but I will need coffee in the morning, and the operative word here is *need*."

He went to the fireplace and struck one of the matches from a box on the mantel. The paper and kindling laid under the logs crackled and lit.

"I doubt you'd find anything open this late," I told him, looking at my watch. My internal clock had taken a vacation, it could have been anything from 6 p.m. to midnight, but my watch said it was 9:30. "Besides, look what happened the last time you went into a grocery store at night. That should put you off shopping forever, if the music in the Food Right hadn't already done it."

He grinned as he stood up, his face lit by the flames leaping around the log on the hearth. "I wonder where they get the stuff they play," he remarked. "The first time I went in I swear I heard the theme from *Jaws* played as a tango."

"My favorite was 'Sheep May Safely Graze' done dance-mix style."

He looked around the room, apparently for lamps. He turned on the one beside the chair where Emily Ann reposed, and another near the love seat. He went to the light switch by the door and switched off the overhead fixture. The room instantly became a cozy nest.

"You're right though," he said, returning to where I was sitting. "I may never go into a store again. I'll have to figure out how to buy groceries on the Internet. Jack, get down now," he added, and with a reproachful look Jack hopped off the couch. Bob took his place beside me. "Good boy." He reached down and gave Jack a scratch on the chest before picking up the two glasses of wine and handing one to me. "Here you go. I doubt if it will hold a candle to my cocoa, but it no doubt is fine in its own way. What should we drink to?"

"I don't know...world peace and dry clothing," I chose at random. We touched the rims of our glasses together and a merry crystalline note chimed out.

The wine was indeed fine, probably the best I'd ever tasted. Ambrose obviously didn't search out the best three dollar merlots that money can buy. I could feel dark red warmth trickling down my throat and spreading to my arms and legs and face. I sank against the back of the couch and took another sip.

"I'm bushed," Bob sighed, leaning back as well and twisting his wineglass in his fingers. Shots of ruby light glinted in the crystal. "For some reason it's hard to relax when you're tied to a chair. I didn't intend to fall asleep in the barn. I sat down to rest and the next thing I knew Jack was giving my face a bath."

"You should go to bed," I told him. He nodded.

"In a bit. I'm tired but I'm so wired I doubt if I'd go to sleep."

"What was it like being kidnapped?"

He looked at me and frowned. "You know, I keep asking myself why I didn't just refuse to go with her when she accosted me in the store. It's unlikely she would have shot me in public, in a grocery store of all places. If it had been Walsh I would have tried to resist. It's hard to explain. She looked desperate. Miserable. This sounds stupid but in a way I wanted to help her out. Or maybe I thought someone who looked that desperate really might shoot me, I don't know." He shook his head.

"You have fine gentlemanly instincts," I told him. "Look how nice you were to that crazy woman who tried to steal your car a couple of weeks ago."

"Yeah, but she had a very handsome dog with her. I can never resist a handsome dog." He sipped some more wine. "One thing about last night..."

"Yes?"

"It didn't seem—*planned*."

"What do you mean?"

"She had rope to tie me up, but a hotel room is an odd place to take someone you've kidnapped. What if I'd done a lot of yelling and people in the adjoining rooms heard? And wouldn't you expect some kind of torture to go along with kidnapping and interrogation?"

I gave a little shudder. "Ig, don't even say that. Think of all the kidnapping stories where they mail off some body part if the ransom isn't paid."

"I admit I'm pretty attached to all my parts. Anyway, if not torture, at least some kind of pressure. All she did was keep asking me where the tape was, and I kept refusing to tell her. Ransom didn't come into the picture at all."

"It does sound like an awfully genteel kidnapping," I said. "I wonder if Ambrose is right, and she and Carl are working at cross purposes."

"Could be, but I'm damned if I know what those purposes could be," he said. "I'm convinced Walsh wants to remove me as a threat to his prosperous lifestyle, but what's her story?"

"I hate not knowing stuff, or at least not having a way to find out."

"I know. Is she an accomplice? Maybe she was an accomplice and he double crossed her. Or vice versa."

"If I had been his accomplice, I'd be looking for something to protect me from becoming his next victim," I said.

"Good point. Ian's stepfather has not exhibited a lot of—what was it?—fine gentlemanly instincts." He took another sip of wine, then set the glass down. A big yawn forced its way out of his mouth. He looked exhausted. I set down my glass beside his.

"You're tired, you need to get some sleep," I repeated.

"First things first, though," he said, and wrapped his arms around me. He kissed my temple, my forehead, then zoned in on my mouth. He tasted like very good wine. I could feel myself start to react very much as I had to the wine, a gentle warmth flowing down all my limbs, a buzz in my head. I hadn't had a kiss like this in a very long time.

Hell, I hadn't had a kiss like this one *ever*.

I discovered my arms had encircled him, and we were leaning into each other. After a long, long time we paused for air. "Louisa," he murmured, coming in for another kiss. One of the voices in my head asked me if I knew what I was doing, if I was ready for this, and did I remember I was in a cabin in the woods with only one bed, but I could barely hear it over the rushing of blood in my ears.

25

The alignment of the stars that day dictated that my fate would turn on the actions of small mammals with long tails.

Fabulous kisses could not distract me from the mouse that ran over us just then. The creature started its foray at Bob's end of the love seat, dashed straight across us, and leapt off my end. Bob jumped and I gave an embarrassing shriek and somehow levitated up onto the couch. Jack bayed, and both dogs gave chase to the rodent, which dashed and zigged all over the cabin, finally disappearing under the stove. Emily Ann tried to dig it out, but the wide boards of the polished floor were unyielding. She remained for some time with her rump in the air and her nose glued to the bottom of the stove. Jack tried back-trailing, sniffing along the mouse's track, which led him on an eccentric path to Bob and me.

The action took less than a minute, but as a spell breaker it was as good as a bucketful of cold water. Bob looked at me standing on the furniture.

"Don't you dare say anything," I warned him. "I can't help it. It's a visceral reaction to small, fast moving objects. Just because I'm acting like a cartoon character does *not* mean this is funny." Embarrassment put a crabby note in my voice.

He contrived to look innocent. "I wasn't going to say a word," he lied. I glared at him. I could tell he was struggling to keep a straight face as he held out his hand to help me descend. I stepped down as haughtily as I could, pretending I wasn't ready to leap back onto the love seat should the mouse be foolish enough to reappear.

The dogs gave up their chase, though I would have preferred that Emily Ann remain at her post by the stove all night, to prevent the mouse's return. The burst of exercise made them think that a trip outside would be a good idea, and they went over to the door and stood looking expectantly at us.

I shot one last look at the stove. "I'll take them out," I said firmly. Bob started to protest. "No, I'll do it. You stand guard and make sure the mouse doesn't come back. We'll just be a couple of minutes."

I leashed the dogs, not wanting them to take off into the woods after some enticing smell or sound. "You guys have had enough hunting for one night," I told them. The creaking porch swayed beneath us. They led me down the steps and across the small yard, away from the direction of the road. I walked about

205

thirty feet from the house to let them accomplish what we'd come out for. We paused, and I looked up at the sky. The storm clouds of this morning had blown away, and a million stars gleamed overhead, so intense away from town where no lights clouded their brilliance.

I took a deep breath of chilly night air. Behind me loomed a cabin with a man in it that I liked a whole lot, and only one bed. We'd had two perfectly wonderful kisses. And I was scared. I could remind myself over and over that Bob was not Roger, and that Roger was dead; but even if there are no ghosts, the dead still can haunt us.

I don't know how long I stood shivering in the night. Long enough for Emily Ann to finish following her nose around the circle allowed by her six foot leash, and to come and lean against the back of my legs. She was so tall that her head curved around my hip at waist height. Jack too gave up exploring the ground, and came to sit in front of me.

"So, pups, what do you think?"

Emily Ann yawned.

I inhaled, smelling damp leaves and wood smoke. "You're right," I told her. "It's time for bed. Let's go." We trooped through the yard, up the creaking steps and across the porch. I opened the door and stepped inside.

I didn't see Bob at first. The light from the fire was dim, and he had left on a single lamp. Before I could panic over his disappearance a rather loud snore came from the bed. He was lying on top of the covers.

His shoes were neatly lined up by the bedside table, and his shirt and jeans folded and placed on the floor. He was still wearing a tee shirt and boxers and socks.

I unleashed the dogs. Emily Ann climbed back onto her chosen chair. Jack went over and nuzzled Bob's hand, which was hanging over the side of the bed. Bob didn't move, and after a second nuzzle Jack walked to the fireplace and curled up in the glow from the fire.

I decided I should get Bob under the covers. It was warm enough now, but in October the room would grow cold before morning.

Moving him wasn't easy. Kidnapping at gunpoint, a night with no sleep, and half a glass of good wine had done him in. I shoved him to one side to get the covers and sheet out from under him, then I arranged his legs under the linens. One arm kept falling off the edge of the bed and dangling. By the time I had him tucked in, I was wide awake and out of breath. I sat down on the love seat to finish my wine. Maybe I should sleep here, I thought, ignoring the fact that the love seat was several inches shorter than me and that either my head or my feet or both would hang off the ends. I remembered the mouse, and shook my head.

Yes, I was scared to climb into that high four poster bed with a man I hadn't known very long.

But I was more scared of that damned mouse.

At last I rose to get ready for bed, carrying a canvas bag into the bathroom that Kay had packed with some necessities. I unzipped the bag and pulled a long silk night dress out of the bag. I'd never seen this

207

garment before. The chandelier gleamed on its lace and tucks and yards and yards of almost-sheer fabric. Kay had raided her own dresser drawers instead of packing the old knee-length tee shirt I keep at her place to sleep in. "Kay, you wretch," I muttered, letting the gossamer fabric slide through my hands.

Closing the door, I started to unbutton my jeans. Movement opposite made me stop. The entire room, including me and the chandelier, was reflected in the glass wall separating me from the darkness beyond. One of the voices in my head said chattily, "Gosh, that looks just like a one way mirror."

Another one added, "Yeah, could be bleachers full of spectators. They're going to love your strip show."

"Don't be ridiculous," I snapped back, "nothing is out there but empty woods. Nobody's watching."

I went over to the glass wall and tried to peer out. The reflections made it impossible. I turned back to the door, opened it a few inches, and turned off the chandelier. In a moment my eyes adjusted to the dim light coming from the other room. The reflections were gone from the window. I went over and peered out again, seeing only a tangle of trees in the light of a frosty moon that had just cleared their tops. Nothing moved that I could see, so I stripped off the jeans and sweater I had put on hours or days ago. My bra joined the pile. Kay's silly nightie slid over my head with a silken whisper.

This garment was so voluminous that anyone could have worn it. The length hit me a few inches above my ankles, though on Kay it would have been close to the floor. I felt more ready for a costume party than for bed. All I needed, I thought, was a pair of fluffy high heeled mules, a tiara and a lorgnette and I'd be ready for Mardi Gras—or to run a high class brothel.

Crossing the room yet again, I turned the light back on, blinking in the brightness. I fished a toothbrush and toothpaste out of the bag and did my teeth, brushing long enough to remove a layer of enamel along with any lingering plaque. I rinsed the brush and laid it by the sink. I opened the medicine cabinet to see what Ambrose kept in it. It was as bare as the one at Bob's house. The men of my acquaintance seemed singularly healthy. As I closed the mirrored door I noticed some water spots on the glass. I got a wad of toilet paper and polished them away. My reflection in the mirror showed that my hair was in disarray. I found a hairbrush in the bag and started brushing. The bristles felt good against my scalp. I closed my eyes and kept brushing. After a while I realized I was counting strokes. Forty-two, forty-three...had I reverted to being a pioneer woman, giving my hair its hundred strokes before going to bed?

Ah. Yes. Going to bed.

I know that many women would climb into bed beside a man they hadn't known long without a second thought. I suspected that if I didn't like Bob so much I wouldn't be so diffident. That liking made the stakes too high. But the alternative of staying up all night was impossible, and the sofa was too short, and a pile of sofa cushions on the floor would render me too accessible to the mouse. It would have to be the bed.

The main room of the cabin was quiet. Bob had turned onto his side and was no longer snoring, but appeared just as soundly asleep. Jack had managed to get up onto the high bed and was a nearly perfect circle at Bob's feet. Emily Ann blinked sleepily at me and thumped her tail on her chair when I crossed the room to caress her head and to turn off the lamp by the sofa.

I put another log onto the remains of the fire and heaped some coals around it. Little blue flames erupted. My feet had gotten cold in the bathroom, and I held my toes toward the warmth of the flames. Jack jumped down from the bed with a thump. He came and leaned against my leg and stared into the fire with me.

"Go to bed," I finally muttered at myself. I must have said it out loud; both dogs looked up. "Sorry, guys," I whispered, "go to sleep."

Jack turned and hopped onto the love seat and curled up with his nose over his flank.

I crossed the room to the bed and turned back the covers on the side opposite the sleeping Bob. The steps for climbing onto the high mattress were on his side, but I figured I could scramble up without them.

If I hadn't been wearing that silk nightie I might have made it, but the bed was too high. I stepped back to look at it. How utterly ridiculous that I couldn't get a knee securely up there. I turned my back, put my hands on the mattress, and gave a hop, but I slithered back down. I turned back and grasped the covers to pull myself up but they shifted toward me, leaving Bob partially bare. I went around to get the steps. They weighed a ton. I could barely budge them. They appeared to be made of wood, but felt like they had been cast from cement. I tried pushing them, but they made a loud scraping noise on the wooden floor that had both dogs awake and alert. I stopped trying to move the steps to consider other options.

Maybe I could get Bob to roll over to the other side, I thought. A tentative nudge had no effect. I pushed. No reaction. Remembering how hard it had been to get him where he was in the first place, I wouldn't have put good odds on my chances of moving him another two feet.

I could either climb over Bob or sleep on the love seat. I tried to remember if I'd seen more blankets in the closet, and could only picture sheets and towels. I would freeze. I was already cold. The wooden floorboards sucked body heat right out through the bottoms of my feet.

And once it was quiet, that mouse could come out from under the stove.

I decided I no longer cared who was in that bed. It was late, I was cold, and I wanted under those covers. Resolutely I mounted the three steps, put a knee beside Bob on the mattress and my hands on the other side of him and started to lever myself over his body. As I brought the other foot off the steps, he turned his head and mumbled something. I froze, balanced precariously. My heart accelerated at the thought that Bob would wake and see me suspended over him, on display in Kay's nightgown.

He gave a groan, moving one hand up to his chin. Deep, even breaths resumed. The leg I held aloft started to tremble so I eased it over his body and onto the bed. I shifted my weight to bring the other leg along and that's when I got tangled with the nightgown and went sprawling.

Bob can really sleep. I had to put my hands on his chest and push to get my face off the quilt. He mumbled again, brought the hand from under his chin to my thigh, and rolled toward the center of the bed. It was enough to change my center of gravity and I rolled across him to the other side. He began to snore again as I worked my way free of the muffling folds of silk.

After another tussle with the blankets I got myself between the sheets, hoping for warmth and finding icy cold. I inched toward Bob. He radiated body heat, and I sneaked my freezing feet closer to his legs. Tentatively I touched him with my toes. He didn't move. I rolled closer and pressed the icy bottoms of both feet firmly against his calves. The breath I'd been holding came out in a quiet "Ahhh." Bob's warmth flowed into my soles, up my legs and radiated out to the rest of my body. I fell asleep.

26

It must have been the birds that woke me. It was barely dawn, and every tree in the woods was filled with every kind of bird, singing every kind of birdsong. The noise was amazing, a wild cacophony. I didn't know so many birds were left in the world.

I became aware next of the scent of lavender and the unfamiliar feel of the pillowcase under my cheek. The angle of the light seemed odd. It took a moment to remember that I was at Ambrose's cabin. I was on my side facing away from Bob. He was spooned around me, pressed up close, one arm circled under my breasts. My breath caught in my throat, then went out in a long sigh. This actually felt pretty good. I relaxed into him. My heart accelerate when he kissed the back of my neck.

"I think I fell asleep," he murmured. "I remember taking off my shoes but nothing after that."

I twisted my neck to peek at him over my shoulder. "You definitely fell asleep," I told him.

"If this is a dream, don't wake me up." He snuggled his whiskery chin against my neck.

"You must have been worn out. You slept like a stone."

"Being kidnapped is a wearing business."

"I've always said that."

"But I think I've recovered. A good night's sleep is a wonderful thing."

"Very restorative," I agreed, and felt myself blush. I turned my face away and moved toward the side of the bed to get up.

"Louisa, come back," he said gently.

I hesitated, then turned onto my back and looked at him. I felt my hair standing up in tufts, and the silk nightgown bunched up under my hips. It wasn't possible that I knew this person well enough to be where I was, yet here indeed I was. But as soon as I raised my eyes to look into his, my fears and hesitations all evaporated. The image of Roger that lived in my head could not be overlaid on this man; no points matched. My arms went around Bob as I continued turning into his embrace.

Some women can talk about what happens in the privacy of their bed. I've known a few, and listened with amazement at the things they would tell. I could no more be that way than I could fly like the birds still singing outside our window.

And yet...

When we were done, I felt I could fly up into the sky like one of the robins or wrens that had wakened me with their songs.

27

"Coffee," he moaned, lying back on his pillow and closing his eyes. Even though he was moaning a large smile hovered on his narrow face.

I grinned back at him. "Addictions are hard to hide. Maybe you could see a hypnotherapist about this." He poked me in the ribs and I giggled. I actually giggled. I was glad Kay wasn't here. She would never let me hear the end of it. Well, I was glad she wasn't here for several reasons. Thank heavens for stubborn women who always get their own way.

"Have you no vices, woman?" he asked, sitting up and pulling part of the sheet around his shoulders. The air in the cabin was chilly with the fire out. His hair was standing on end and he had stubble on his chin, and he looked wonderful. And to be honest, that stubble had proved interestingly invigorating.

"No, none at all," I replied airily. "Unless you consider orange juice a vice, and I'm in luck because I think I saw a can in the freezer when you were looking

215

for cocoa last night. In fact, far from having vices, I'd say I have a number of virtues. I'm loyal, amusing, and turn around three times before lying down."

"Oh, I would say you have more virtues than that." He waggled his eyebrows at me in comic suggestiveness. "But orange juice—now that is certainly a vice. You just lucked out that it's a vice that can be frozen. Ambrose is definitely the kind of guy who would know that coffee needs to be fresh. I bet he brings his own beans every time he comes out here."

"Just shows how much you know about orange juice," I countered. "Fresh squeezed and frozen are as different as instant coffee and some froufrou brew from an expensive beanery. But *I* know what is proper in a rural cabin, where one sheds one's urban airs and affectations to embrace bucolic simplicity and drink whatever one finds on the premises."

"Yeah, like eighty dollar bottles of wine."

"Yeah, like that."

We smiled at each other.

Emily Ann appeared at his side of the bed, pressing her muzzle onto the mattress and giving us a Princess-Di look through her short lashes. She wanted to go out. Jack came over beside her and put his front paws on the mattress, his body swaying with his wag.

"Okay, Emily Ann, you and Jack have been very patient," Bob told her. "Give me just a minute." He turned and gave me a lingering kiss before sliding out of bed. He gathered up his clothes from the floor and disappeared into the bathroom. A few minutes later he was back, clothed and reaching for the leashes. When they had gone outside, I leaned off the bed and rummaged around on the floor for that nightgown. It had been flung just out of reach. I stretched out and out and had almost snagged it when I began to slide off the bed head-first. I clutched at the sheets and teetered on the edge. With a wriggle I managed to roll back onto the mattress. I looked quickly toward the door to make sure I hadn't been observed, pulled in a lungful of air, gave a little shrug, and leaped out of bed.

The floor was even colder than it had been last night, and the unheated air was brisk. I grabbed the nightie and slipped it over my head. I took a couple of steps toward the fireplace to see if there was any chance of an easy fire. The embers appeared to be out.

I was looking around for some kindling when I heard Bob's voice outside. I assumed he was talking to the dogs—but then I realized another male voice was answering back. I scooted over to the window and looked out. Ambrose was sitting in his car talking to Bob through the open window. As I watched he climbed out and shook hands with Bob. He held a videocassette in the other hand.

I started to go to the door and wave to him, but realized in time that I was not dressed to receive callers. I dashed to the bathroom, dashed out to grab my clothes, and back in again.

I dithered. I wanted a shower before I got dressed, but should I do without and get dressed and go say hello to Ambrose? I'd had the kind of morning activity one needed to shower after. But it was Ambrose's cabin, would it be too rude not to go out?

The shower won. I started running water in the tub. In the morning light, the glass wall looked out across a short strip of lawn and a line of trees. When the water was hot and streaming through the shower head, I flung off the gown and jumped into the tub, pulling the vinyl-lined curtains together. I sighed as hot water cascaded over my shoulders and back.

In a few minutes I heard a knock at the door. "Yes?" I called out. "I'm in the shower."

I poked my head out between the shower curtains and saw Bob peeking around the door. "Louisa, Ambrose is here. He was able to get the tape already. I was planning to run into that town for coffee, but maybe I should wait to play the tape for you." He stepped into the bathroom and pulled the door mostly shut.

"Ambrose didn't bring coffee?"

"No, and he did apologize. He's waiting on the porch until you're dressed. He suggested that we go for provisions. Do you want us to wait so you can come along? Or shall we bring back stuff for breakfast?"

"If you don't mind I'll stay here and wallow in the shower for a bit," I told him. "But are you sure you have to go out of my sight? The last time we had a conversation like this you ended up getting kidnapped."

"True. Maybe we could talk Ambrose into going and I could stay here and watch you shower. When I go into fits of caffeine withdrawal you could leap out of the tub to revive me." He waggled his eyebrows again.

"Perhaps you had better go along to town. My first aid skills are rudimentary at best."

"Practice could help them."

"Just watch out for the bad guys, would you? I'm not up for any more forays into the woods."

"I'll be careful," he promised. "It shouldn't take long. Ambrose knows the place so we won't waste any time."

"Okay."

"I'll take Jack along for the ride. What about Emily Ann?"

"You can leave her with me, but hurry back."

"Oh, I will definitely hurry back." He came closer and leaned toward me to give my wet lips a quick kiss, and another lingering one. Finally he turned and left the room.

I looked at the door he'd disappeared through, then pulled my head back inside the shower curtains. I'd never seen the brand of shampoo in the shower before, but it was thick and amber colored and smelled wonderful. I piled my sudsy hair as high as its short length would allow, and let hot water rain on my shoulders and back while I drifted off in thoughts of Bob, his warmth and kindness and prickly whiskers.

When at last I felt sufficiently parboiled I peeked out to make sure no boy scout troops were hiking past the window. I had showered long enough for steam to cloud the glass, giving an other-worldly fog to the forest beyond.

I climbed out, wrapped up in one of the large, luxurious bath towels, and started to towel my hair. In my distraction I had neglected to rinse out the shampoo. Back into the tub to rinse, out again to dry and dress.

Orange juice was next on my agenda, but in the kitchen area, I saw the tape lying on the counter. The box was neatly lettered in Bob's hand, "Ian Walsh—Copy." The cassette, when I tipped out, had an identical label. I hadn't noticed a television last night, but now I looked around. An armoire sat at an angle in the corner, between the windows on the front and side of the cabin. I walked over and opened the cabinet, and found a TV with a built-in VCR. I pushed in the tape, picked up the remote control, and walked back over to the kitchen area.

I pried out the can of orange juice welded by frost to the freezer. A cut glass pitcher was in a cabinet next to a row of crystal tumblers. I felt a goofy smile on my face as I stirred and thought about Bob. Soon that first lovely swallow trickled across my tongue and down my throat. Coffee could never be as good as this.

I set down the tumbler, picked up the remote and clicked to start the tape. A certain amount of fumbling was required before I could figure out how to turn up the sound. Bob was not in the picture but as the volume came up I heard his voice talking in a soothing tone.

"—a session with Ian Walsh. We have had three previous sessions. Ian is working toward hypnotic anesthesia for dental surgery. Today we will be testing the depth of his trance with temporal regressions."

I took another sip of juice. On the screen I saw a young man, compactly built, with blonde hair and a slightly darker mustache and small beard that had the effect of making him look younger than his nineteen years. He was stretched out on a leather-upholstered chaise. His eyes were closed and he looked very relaxed. I studied his face, and liked what I saw. I felt a stab of hot anger that he was dead.

I turned to throw away the empty can, and heard a car outside. Emily Ann jumped off the love seat and ran over to the door. "That didn't take them long," I remarked. "I wonder if Bob or Ambrose forgot something."

I meant to click the stop button on the remote but managed to hit the pause instead. Ian's image froze on the screen, eyes closed but evidently speaking, his lips forming a word. I left it, hurrying across the room to throw open the door.

I expected to see Kay's sleek red Mitsubishi that we had borrowed last night for the drive up here, or perhaps Ambrose's Infiniti. Instead I saw a gray Mercedes.

The driver's door opened.

The woman in red got out.

221

28

My breath whooshed out in an audible gasp. The passenger door opened and my cousin emerged. She saw me in the open doorway and waved. "Lou, don't panic, it's okay," she yelled.

Then the back passenger-side door opened and Ed Johnson, Willow Falls Chief of Police, crawled out, blinking. I stared at the car, half expecting more people to come tumbling out as though this were a clown car in a circus. Ed scowled as he flexed his shoulders and stretched. He looked at his wrist, but wasn't wearing a watch, and that made him scowl more. Kay turned and said something I couldn't hear across the top of the car to the other woman. Emily Ann started out the door. I grabbed her collar and held on as the three approached the porch.

"Geez, what a dump," Ed said.

Kay paused to glare at him. "There you go, judging things by what they look like."

He threw up his hands and growled, "Sorry! What it looks like is all I have to go on so far."

She turned her back on him and led the way up the creaking steps and across the porch. I held my breath that the quaking structure would not collapse with the three of them standing on it. I backed into the room, still gripping Emily Ann's collar. Kay and the other woman entered. Ed clumped in after a final disbelieving glare at the front of the cabin.

The blonde woman had on the same jeans and red plaid shirt she'd worn when she drove away in my car. She still possessed the beauty I'd first seen across a rain-swept parking lot, but up close her face was older than I expected, and she looked tired and worried. Faint dark smudges stained the skin under her deep blue eyes, and her lips were held in a thin line.

I looked from her to Kay. "What are you all doing here?" I demanded. "Did Ed arrest this woman?"

No one answered me. Kay had stopped two steps into the room, and the other two bunched awkwardly behind her. Kay's eyes took in all the details of the cabin's interior. Her gaze alighted on the still-tumbled sheets and covers on the enormous bed. She looked back at me with one eyebrow slightly raised.

"See, I was right, it is better inside than out," she said, looking from me to Ed. My hand itched to give her a good smack, but I knew she would only laugh.

Ed grunted in reply. He crossed the room and sat on the arm of one of the chairs. He looked annoyed enough to assist me in anything I might want to do to

Kay. He was very rumpled; his jeans and shirt appeared to have come directly from the bottom of a closet, his hair hadn't seen a comb, and if he'd shaved in recent memory, it hadn't been this morning. If he'd looked this angry the day they broke up, I suspected Kay had been lucky to get off with only a ticket for littering.

"What are you doing here?" I asked again. I couldn't help how rude it sounded.

Kay turned to me and gestured toward the blonde. "Louisa, I want you to meet Bonnie Becker," she replied, "Ian's aunt."

I gaped. "Ian's aunt?"

The woman nodded. "I am so sorry for barging in on you. I have a lot of explaining to do," she said. Her voice was low in both pitch and volume.

"Where's Bob?" Kay asked.

"Gone for coffee," I told her, "and other provisions."

"Did he walk? My car is still outside," she said, looking puzzled.

"No, Ambrose has already been here. They went in his car. There's not much food here other than some orange juice, a box of expensive crackers, and some very good wine, any of which you are welcome to."

"That's okay, we had breakfast at my house," Kay assured me. "Well, Bonnie and I did. I don't think Ed has had anything."

"Yeah, like enough sleep," he growled.

"You had breakfast?" I burst out. How cozy. First the woman kidnaps Bob and then she breakfasts with Kay.

"This is all so crazy," the woman—Bonnie—said. She looked earnestly at me. "I found your business cards in your car, and went to OKay Antiques last night looking for Mr. Richardson. Kay recognized me and made me listen to his side of the story." Her eyes fell. "I can hardly bear the thought of facing him. I hope he'll forgive me for my stupidity. You see, I thought he was working with my former brother-in-law."

"Carl's housekeeper found out he had the original tape, and she told Bonnie about it," Kay took up the tale. "But they thought that Bob had been involved with Carl, or had kept a copy to cover his own ass, or maybe for blackmail. Georgia, the housekeeper, listened in on the extension whenever Carl was on the phone at the house. Apparently he hired a detective to find out where Bob went when he left High Cross, and Georgia was able to tell Bonnie so she got here first and found Bob and carted him off."

"Wait, wait, wait," I said. "Hold it. That went by too fast."

"I'll second that," said Ed. "Housekeeper? Detective?"

Kay gave us both an exasperated look. She hates to slow down. "Okay, in words of one syllable—"

"There's nothing wrong with our vocabularies," said Ed, "we just need more words spoken slower."

He and I looked at each other. I wouldn't have sworn to it, but I thought I detected a glimmer of humor in his eyes.

Kay glared at both of us but decided not to pursue this line of conversation. "All right, polysyllabic but slow." She began to prowl around the cabin as she talked. "Bonnie and I talked a long time last night—"

"All night," Bonnie put in.

"—and here's what we think happened. Bob stashed the original tape of Ian's hypnosis session in his safety deposit box.

"But he kept a duplicate," Bonnie said.

"He went to see the police detective, who acted as though he thought Bob's accusation of Carl was ridiculous. But Bonnie tells me that Carl is politically well-connected in High Cross—"

"He was on the city council for a while, until he figured out some work was involved," Bonnie explained.

"He also donates money to some police charity and golfs with the chief and all that good old boy stuff. So we think Bob's idea that the detective told Carl about the tape is likely. Or if the detective didn't tell Carl directly, he told someone within the police who's connected to Carl. Within a day or so of Bob's visit to the police, Carl knew the tape existed, and that it was in a safety deposit box in the bank that he owns. I don't know how he got into Bob's box, but he'd have complete access to all bank records and somehow he did it. We know he had the original tape, because his housekeeper—"

"That would be Georgia," Ed said to me.

"—Georgia was in the house when he was playing the tape. She was setting the table in the dining room for a dinner party he was having the next day, and she heard Ian's voice. She followed the sound and saw Carl in his den watching the tape."

"And how did we come to know all this?" Ed inquired. I let go of Emily Ann's collar and crossed to the love seat, perching on its overstuffed arm. This could take some time.

"Because Georgia called me," Bonnie replied. "She was upset, and she was afraid."

"Who wouldn't be?" said Kay.

"She heard enough of the tape to realize the implications, that Carl had murdered my sister Pru and Ian. She started working for my sister when Pru was married to Ian's father, long before Carl was in the picture. She helped raise Ian and was devastated when he died."

"So when she realized Carl had killed them, she got in touch with Bonnie," Kay said.

Bonnie continued, "Georgia knew Carl is connected to the police and she was afraid to go to them. We never got a chance to watch the tape. He hid it or destroyed it. But Georgia began to listen to Carl's phone calls whenever she could do it safely. We know Carl hired detectives because he had them call him at home to report what they'd found."

"Wait a minute," I said, feeling suddenly indignant. "Why would you think that Bob was on Carl's side?"

"We misinterpreted something Georgia heard. Carl was on the phone to the detective. She picked up the phone a few seconds after their conversation started, and Carl was saying what a good thing it was that 'he' had brought the tape straight to him, but that there could be a copy of it. They were speculating on whether this person might try blackmail. We thought they were talking about the person who made the tape."

"But they must have meant someone in the police." Kay's pacing brought her next to Bonnie. "If one of the cops wanted to blackmail him, making a copy of this tape would be a dandy place to start."

Bonnie sighed and shook her head. "I have been out of my mind these weeks since Ian died. I jumped to the conclusion that it was Bob they were talking about. A few days later Georgia heard the detective tell Carl where Bob was staying. I got in my car and drove to Willow Falls. I still can't believe I actually kidnapped him." She shot a worried look at Ed. "It was just chance that I saw him going into that grocery store. I had been at the home warehouse next to it buying rope because I had some crazy idea of sneaking up on him in his house."

"But how did you recognize him?" Ed asked.

She looked surprised. "I went to him for hypnosis, years ago, when I was having trouble quitting smoking."

"That's why Ian went to Bob," Kay said. "His aunt recommended it."

"He didn't recognize me. I was afraid he would, but I looked a lot different then."

Bonnie paused, and her eyes filled with tears. She shook her head once. "I *have* been out of my mind.

228

I'm sure that he—that scum—" she struggled with her voice, "—that vile Carl Walsh killed my sister and my nephew. I loved them both. I will do *anything* to see that he gets what he deserves."

The way she said his name sent a chill scurrying down my back. I glanced in Ed's direction, and saw that he was watching Bonnie with his eyes narrowed. Emily Ann left my side and went over and leaned on Bonnie, peering up into her face. Bonnie's hand settled gently on Emily Ann's head. You could see her relax a fraction.

Then she looked past me and saw the television screen and froze. The blood drained from her face and she swayed. I thought she was going to fall, but she sagged against Emily Ann, who stood firm. I jumped up to help her, but Ed was faster. He was at her side, but she waved him off as she straightened again.

"Where did you get that?" Bonnie demanded, pointing.

Kay looked around wildly and saw the TV. "Oh, god, is that—"

"It's the tape, Bob's copy, the one we've been looking for."

For the first time Ed looked fully awake. He took a couple of steps toward the TV and looked hard at the image of Ian. "Have you watched it yet?" he growled at me.

I shook my head and said to Bonnie, "I'm sorry, Ambrose was here and left the video and I just stuck it in the machine a minute ago. Let me turn it off."

She gave her head a little shake. "It was seeing

him...Oh, I miss him so much!" Her voice quavered. She pressed a hand to her mouth and blinked hard.

I stepped over to the armoire and hit the power button on the television. The screen went dark. I pushed the eject button and pulled the tape out, looking blankly at the label. Finally I crossed the room and laid the tape on the kitchen counter next to my glass of juice.

"I think we should watch it," Ed said. "Put it back in the machine."

At the same time Kay asked again, "Where did Bob and Ambrose go?"

I turned to her. "We saw a grocery store at that little town at the crossroads about fifteen miles back. He and Ambrose have gone to pick up food," I told her. "They must have taken Ambrose's car. You may have passed them on your way here. I don't think they had been gone very long when you arrived, but I was in the shower. I'm not sure how long it's been."

"Ah," Kay nodded, knowing my showering habits. "I wasn't paying attention to cars going the other way," she confessed. "You know what?"

"What," I obliged.

"I think we should all watch the tape together. I'll follow Ambrose and Bob. I'm sure I can find them, and I'll get them to hustle their butts back here."

"But—" I started to object.

"If they arrive and see Bonnie's car, Bob will either take off again or barrel in here thinking he needs to save you, Louisa."

I nodded.

"Which car should I take? Bonnie, I'd better take yours, in case I miss them on the road and they get back before me. In the meantime tell Louisa more about what we talked about last night."

Bonnie nodded. She was still pale but had recovered her composure. She held out a ring of keys with her left hand. A gold fob engraved with the letter B dangled among the keys.

Kay took the ring and started for the door. "I'll be back as soon as I can," she said over her shoulder.

"Wait a minute," Ed said. He stood up from the arm of the chair he'd been slumped on. "You dragged me out of bed to see this tape. Get back here and let's watch the blasted thing."

She glared at him. "I got you out of bed because we need your help. We're after a murderer, remember?"

"Alleged murderer," he said. I held my breath, hoping he wouldn't call her 'lady.' Kay continued before he had a chance to.

"We need someone official to get this guy behind bars. If you can't wait for Bob and Ambrose, watch the tape with Louisa and Bonnie. But I don't see what difference a few more minutes is going to make." She turned again and started out the door.

"I'm coming with you. Give me the keys."

"No." She stopped to scowl at him. "I can find Bob and Ambrose without you."

"You can, but you're not going to."

Kay spun around and was out the door. He followed her. I was amazed that anyone so rumpled and sleepy-looking could move so fast. Bonnie and I hurried out to the front porch. Kay had the engine started and the car moving.

"All right, you can drive," Ed said as he jerked open the passenger door and threw himself inside. She executed a tight three point turn and sped down the drive to the road. I could hear their voices over the sound of the car. Ed waved his hands to emphasize whatever point Kay was not listening to. The Mercedes turned onto the road and disappeared. The sound of the engine faded into the distance.

I looked at Bonnie. She blinked.

"Goodness, what a pair. Your cousin is, um, a forceful woman," she commented.

"My cousin is hell on wheels," I told her, "but she's also one of the best people I know."

"She made me stay at her place and we ended up talking most of the night. This morning she decided we needed official help, so she went to Ed's house and woke him up and made him come with us."

"That sounds like her. I wonder how she got past his mother."

"He'll arrest me as soon as Mr. Richardson gets back and says he wants to press charges." She looked sad and tired and resigned.

"You're lucky she only made you spend the night. She's capable of anything. You could have ended up racing back to High Cross to kidnap Carl."

"Don't think we didn't consider that," she admitted.

"I can't speak for Bob, but I don't think he's all

that mad at you. He did say it was a very polite kidnapping. And what man wouldn't want to be kidnapped by a beautiful blonde?"

"Yeah, right," she scoffed, but a small smile curved her mouth. The sunshine bathing the cabin's porch lit her face.

Realization dawned. "Bonnie," I said slowly, "do you know what you did?"

"What?" Her brow puckered in concern.

"You saved Bob's life."

"What do you mean?"

"You got him out of the way at just the right moment. I don't think Carl showed up at his house at dawn the next morning just wanting to say hello, do you?"

Her eyes widened. "You're right. Carl is desperate to hide his crimes. The stakes get higher with each murder."

"He'll be furious when he finds out what you did. He probably thought he could sneak over to Willow Falls, find Bob and quietly kill him, maybe even hide the body or make it look like another suicide, and get away with murder once more."

"That sounds like him."

"And you waltzed in, scooped Bob out of a grocery store, and hid him away where he was safe. I don't think Bob's going to be mad, I think he's going to be kissing your feet. I think you should have business cards printed—Bonnie Becker, Deus ex Machina."

A real smile lit her face for the first time. "Wouldn't that be Dea?"

I laughed. "Hey, you want to come in and have some orange juice?"

She nodded. "Love to. It would feel so—so normal to drink orange juice."

I started into the cabin. Her sudden intake of breath stopped me in my tracks. I turned to see her staring toward the road, body rigid and eyes wide. Following her gaze I saw a big black car sliding down the drive. It was driven by a man, a large man I had last seen searching my car in front of Bob's house.

Carl.

Here.

29

"Oh. My. God," Bonnie breathed. We jumped into the house and I slammed and locked the door. "He followed us here. He must have found your cards and Kay's shop."

"He would have been watching her place when you left." I said. "And when Kay and Ed drove off just now..."

"We've got to get out of here," Bonnie gasped, looking around wildly.

I peered through the small panes of glass in the top half of the front door. The black car stopped and Carl climbed out. He took a leisurely look around before he turned toward the cabin.

"Quick, into the bathroom," I told Bonnie.

She gave me a confused look. "What? You want to hide in the bathroom?" She clearly thought I was insane.

"No, that's where the back door is. Come on," I threw over my shoulder as I hastened across the room.

She followed. I tugged back the deadbolt on the outside door and tried to turn the knob. Still locked. A twist of the inset button and we had the door open. As Bonnie and Emily Ann crowded through, I remembered the tape. It was on the kitchen counter. If I left it, we'd have no concrete evidence that Carl had killed his wife or her son.

I dashed back into the cabin. The porch step creaked as it took Carl's weight. Perhaps he was unsure it would hold him; a pause before the next creak gave me time to flee back into the bathroom. I slammed and locked the door I'd just come through, and lunged for the one leading outside. I took a moment to twist the lock button in the knob—if he came around and tried to get in this way, it wouldn't keep him out for long, but it might buy us a little time. And if he made it in the front door and into the bathroom, well, it would give us one more second to run away.

I looked around for Bonnie and Emily Ann. I had a half-formed idea that we could creep around the house and steal Carl's car while he was breaking in. Anything to avoid another woodland chase scene. But Bonnie had already dashed across the yard toward the woods, and I couldn't call out to her to stop without alerting Carl. So, tape in hand, I followed.

It was easy at first. A path of shredded bark wound between the trees behind the cabin, and the underbrush was cut back and thinned, creating a pleasant place for a stroll. I ran down the path. The soft footing muffled my pounding steps.

The rocky terrain dipped and rose among the

trees. A couple of minutes of running took me out of sight of the cabin. A couple more minutes and I was out of the nicely cleared part of the woods and into the usual sort: bushes and brambles and vines and trees with low branches to brain you as you ran.

Ahead of me I caught glimpses of Bonnie and my dog. The woman ran like a gazelle. Of course. Emily Ann coursed beside her, circled back to me, then back to Bonnie. Even as I panted along I thought what a lovely picture they made together, gliding through the woods with flickers of morning sun gleaming on their shoulders. Nothing seemed to touch them as they ran.

I huffed and puffed, struggling to get past the blackberry vines that clawed at my legs. I tripped over a rock hidden by a scraggle of grass and careened into a tree trunk, managing to hold the tape aloft so it didn't get smashed. I felt a sharp pang as something in my back twisted, but somehow I stayed on my feet and ran on.

As I struggled along I thought, I didn't get to finish my orange juice, and now I'm being chased by that same murdering sleazebag banker through more blasted woods. I felt decidedly put-upon. Bonnie and Emily Ann disappeared into a dip in the land, and I stopped to catch my breath. While I stood panting, I reached around and tucked the videocassette into the waistband of my jeans in back under my sweater, as I'd seen waiters in fancy restaurants do with their order pads.

I heard something crash through the woods behind me.

At once I found I had enough breath to run again. I followed the others into the dip and was met by my dog, running back to see where I was. Bonnie was no longer in sight. The vegetation grew thicker at the bottom, and I discovered a little stream running the length of the hollow. A narrow path followed the stream in both directions. I hesitated, wondering which direction to go. Emily Ann started off upstream, to my left, and I followed. She splashed in and out of the water as we ran.

When I saw a break in the underbrush, I jumped across the stream to head up the other side. Actually, I jumped across most of the stream. My heel landed in gooshy mud and I fell to my knees on the damp earth of the bank.

Before I picked myself up I reached around and to be sure the tape was still secure in my waistband. Then I headed away from the creek. The hill here was much steeper than the way down had been. I was reduced to clawing my way up on my hands and knees at one point, which delighted Emily Ann so much that she gave me a play bow, wagging wildly.

"This is not fun," I told her between clenched teeth. "Running in the woods is not fun when a bad guy is chasing you."

I finally gained the top of the hill and rose to my feet. The woods before me were thick in all directions: closely spaced trees and tangled undergrowth, with vines twisted through both. The leaves on the deciduous trees had turned their fall colors and were tumbling to the ground. As I looked around the morning sun shone through a golden leaf as it fell.

I heard shouting from somewhere to my right, first a man's voice, followed by Bonnie's. My ragged breath caught in my throat, and my hand closed around Emily Ann's collar as she pressed close to my side. I felt a shiver go down her body. I started toward the voices, pushing at a tangle of bushes, and found myself inside the Thicket from Hell.

Small multi-trunked trees, or maybe big bushes, rose a couple of feet higher than my head. For all I knew they actually were myanumma bushes or something equally mythical. Some of their leaves had fallen in the October winds and crunched under my feet, but enough still hung from the twiggy branches to form a screen that kept me from seeing anything more than a few feet ahead. Two or three kinds of vines festooned the bushes. I saw withered blackberries on some, and others had leaves turning red. Poison ivy, said some part of my brain that wanted to retreat to childhood rhymes about leaflets three. I mentally kicked myself back to the present.

I stopped and turned in a circle, looking for the easiest way out. There was none. I pressed on, tearing at the smothering vegetation with both hands. I noticed blood streaming from one palm where the talons on a bramble had torn it. It didn't seem important.

The noise I was making as I beat my way out of the thicket seemed thunderous to my ears, and was compounded by the thudding of my heart, but still I could hear Bonnie's voice ahead of me. I finally dropped down and crawled, using my head to butt my way through the tangled vegetation, and finally saw light ahead. I kept going, and emerged from the thicket to find I was on a precipice. I inched forward to peer over the edge. Emily Ann glued herself to my side like the sticktights I'd picked up as we fled.

I looked down on what must be Parson's Lake, though from here it looked more like a river. I could see both a near and a far bank. This must be a cove on the lake's twisting shoreline. About ten feet this side of the water, Bonnie faced the man we'd seen getting out of his black car by the cabin.

Her fists were clenched and her blonde hair had taken on a life of its own as it became decorated with twigs and leaves on her passage through the woods. She looked like an avenging Druid goddess bent upon the destruction of Evil.

My eyes moved from her to him, and settled on the gleam of the gun in his hand. Definitely not a shiny belt buckle.

"I don't have the tape!" Bonnie shouted. "And if I did you'd still never get it."

He laughed, and the sound made my lip curl. "Bonnie, Bonnie, Bonnie, won't you ever learn I always get what I want?" He sounded amused and indulgent, as though Bonnie were a small child who had stamped her foot at him.

"What I've learned is that you're an impotent, thieving son of a bitch who would do anything for a buck. I will see you in hell, you murderer," she snarled. "Too many people know what you've done, and I will be the one you hear laughing when they put you in the gas chamber, you—"

Her voice was cut off by the blast from the gun. The recoil flung his hand up at the same moment the impact from the bullet spun her around and slammed her to the ground.

In the extravagant silence that followed, I heard a gasp and a strangled cry. Too late, I realized they had come from me. Carl's head snapped around as he looked for the source of the sound. I scooted away from the edge, back among the underbrush and out of his sight.

I sat, shaking, barely able to breathe. This was when I realized that for all our talk of murder, it had only been a story to me. Our cozy discussions over bagels and pizza had been a movie I was acting in. But now I had seen real violence. And I would be next. He was going to kill me too.

Emily Ann nosed my cheek and I looked at her. Sitting here waiting for him to come and shoot me was embarrassingly feeble. I forced myself to take a deep breath and crawled back into the thicket, trying to find a hiding place. I looked over my shoulder and saw that my path was obvious behind me. Crawling was not going to get me away fast enough.

I was stabbed with a sudden longing for Bob. He would be as helpless against an armed psychopath as I was, but two of us might have a better chance of taking him by surprise or overpowering him.

Emily Ann was far better than I at sliding through the brush. Her lean body and short coat gave the brambles nothing to snag. A faint glimmer of hope came to me.

"Emily Ann," I whispered, "come here!" She returned to where I crouched, and I took her face between my hands and looked into her wise brown eyes.

"Emily Ann, go find Bob." Her ears pricked a little at his name. "Go to Bob."

I let go of her. She hesitated for just a moment, touched me once with her nose, and slid away in what I hoped was the direction of the cabin. Her feet made little more noise on the crackling leaves covering the ground than a puff of wind would have done. She'd been out of my sight for less than a minute when I heard the roar of the gun once more.

Oh my god, my sweet Emily Ann—had he shot my dog? The thought froze me in place. She was my heart. If she was dead...

A breeze from the direction of the lake shook the leaves around me, and the rustling made me look around. I had to keep moving, I had to get away. I forced myself to my feet and blundered on, pushing blindly through the accursed trees and vines and bushes. Trying to be quiet. Knowing I was doing a lousy job of it. My heart beating in panic kept me moving but my frightened brain seemed barely able to think about where I was heading.

In perhaps ten minutes I stumbled into a little clearing. I stopped short at the sight of a large man, smiling and pointing a gun at me.

30

It was the first time I had seen Carl up close. Neatly cut dark hair with dramatic gray temples over a handsome mask of a face: gray eyes, regular features, nothing out of place. His progress through the woods had left him no more ruffled than a stroll through a city park would have done.

I bleated as I jerked to a stop. His smile grew larger and more frightening.

"Ah, here you are." His voice purred with satisfaction. "The woman who keeps getting in my way. Well, well, this is nice. In fact this is quite satisfactory. I'll be able to get everything wrapped up this morning after all." He sounded as though he had to run a few errands, a little shopping trip. His eyes glittered like old ice.

"You—you shot Bonnie," I blurted. I hated the shake in my voice because I could see how much it pleased him. The corners of the video cassette tucked into my waistband poked my lower back. The video had slipped down as I ran. I hoped my shirt still hung over it but I didn't want to draw attention to it by checking.

"I did shoot her," he agreed pleasantly, "and you're next. But first I want that tape."

"Tape?" I injected all the innocence I could muster into my voice.

"Yes, the tape. The tape that you grabbed as I looked through the door of that rickety cabin. You left the box for it on the kitchen counter."

I forced some air into my lungs. "I don't have it. I dropped it somewhere in the woods."

"Oh, come, come, my good woman, we both know you have it. Give it to me now."

My good woman? This was even more patronizing than being called lady. "I tell you I don't have it," I insisted. The plastic shell burned a hole in my back.

He shrugged, waving the gun a bit. "It doesn't really matter. I'll find it when you're dead."

I scowled at him. I was afraid, but I was also hot and muddy and out of breath and I felt like most of Burnham Wood was entwined in my hair. It made me cross.

"You know, you can't keep getting away with murder. The odds are not in your favor," I said coldly. "People who have been shot are far less plausible as suicides."

"You and my lovely sister-in-law will be at the bottom of the lake in a few minutes, and no one will ever know I have been here," he said. Smugness oozed from him. "Believe me, I *will* get away with whatever I choose. And if you really did drop the tape, if it's not on you, I shouldn't have any trouble following *your* trail through the woods."

I looked at him standing there so casually, pointing that evil gun at me and unable to resist a schoolboy taunt. Every hair gleamed in place, the knife-sharp creases in his slacks absolutely pristine. Once I noticed them, those creases really annoyed me. They were ostentatious. The man had no sense of what was appropriate attire for chasing people through woods.

That thought led my unruly brain back to the picture of Bonnie crashing to the ground, and the imagined one of Emily Ann being shot. I conjured up Bob—this jerk could keep me from ever seeing Bob again, or hearing him laugh, or feeling him kiss me. To have finally found someone warm and vital and sane and to have my new happiness taken away by this—this arrogant stranger was more than I could bear. I gave my head a shake.

As I did, I had another vision of Carl at his bank denying loans to people who needed them.

I don't know where the words came from.

"I'd like to apply for a small business loan." I was as surprised by my words as he was.

The gun wavered as a variety of expressions played across his face. "What?"

"See, I've always wanted to have my own business." My voice was earnest in the extreme. "It's been my dream for years. I feel positively evangelical about it. I want to have my own business putting in sky-lights."

Skylights? I'd never given a thought to sky-lights in my life. And the thought of me climbing around on a roof with tools was worse than ludicrous. I was babbling. But—and this was a definite plus—he hadn't shot me yet.

"Skylights," he repeated. His voice was puzzled. If he wondered where this was going, well, so did I.

A faint rustle from the bushes caught my attention. The noise was so slight it could have been the breeze, if there had been a breeze. But the air was still. Behind Carl I saw Jack. He was moving stiffly and nearly silently, stalking Carl, his lips pulled back in a snarl, his eyes narrowed in an unblinking gaze of absolute hatred. Sweet, funny Jack with his silky ears and exaggerated body—how could I have known he was hiding a mouth full of carpet knives under his floppy lips?

Keep talking, one of the voices in my head commanded. "So many people live in dark houses," I rambled on, forcing my eyes away from Jack and back to Carl's face. "Light makes such a difference. It changes your whole outlook, not to mention the way it improves your physical health. They've done scientific experiments about it. And not just any light. It has to be pure, natural, organic light—"

"This is the stupidest thing I've ever heard in my life," Carl said. His gun came up, aimed at my chest. At the sound of his voice, Jack sprang. He launched himself as silently as he had crept up on us and he sank those carpet knives in Carl's butt. Carl shrieked in surprise and agony, his arm flew up, and the gun went off.

If a running mouse could make me levitate onto the sofa last night, a gun going off a few feet away—a gun that had just been pointed at me—had the power to make me fly. I launched myself toward Carl, not away, reaching for the gun. At least I started out to fly, but my foot encountered a rock on takeoff and I tripped. I fell heavily against Carl. My hands clutched for the gun. We crashed to the ground. Jack bounded back and whirled around to come at Carl's face. Those long doggy teeth snapped on the air inches from Carl's nose. I gripped his wrist, trying to shake the gun loose, but the bastard wouldn't drop it.

He was taller and stronger than me, but I was on top and my weight was an advantage. And he could not possibly have been as angry as I was. He tried to roll over, but Jack was everywhere he turned his face, snapping and growling. We writhed on the ground. I panted, "Drop it, damn it, drop it. *Drop it!*"

The tape popped out of my waistband and clattered to the ground. Our struggle paused as we both stared at the tape. Then he began to fight harder. A few more seconds of struggle and he would break loose. He'd shoot me and Jack and grab the tape and he would win. He would dump our bodies in the lake, and go back to his comfortable life. He would find some way to take Bob out of the picture.

I was not going to let that happen. Perhaps Jack inspired me.

247

I bit him.

The man tasted vile but I savored the savage satisfaction of grinding my teeth into the bones of his wrist. I think I was growling.

Carl bellowed in pain and rage and the gun fell. I grabbed it and shoved myself back onto my knees and then to my feet. I pointed the evil thing at him. Good. I liked this. A gun was way better than a belt buckle.

"Jack, watch him," I commanded. The dog crouched, poised to attack. I reached down and picked up the videocassette, never taking my eyes or the gun off the monster at my feet.

Carl made a move to get up, and my back stiffened with outrage. "Don't even *think* about moving," I told him. My voice was clear and as steady as the gun in my hand. "I know you killed your wife and Ian, and I saw you kill Bonnie. And if you shot my dog, I'm going to kill you myself, you son of a bitch."

My tone must have sounded as convincing to him as it did to me. He subsided onto the ground, and that's when the Mounties arrived.

31

"Then what happened?" Bonnie was enthralled by our tale.

Kay and Bob and I clustered in her hospital room. Flowers were everywhere. She had spent days in the ICU, surrounded by medical machinery, but after she was out of danger she'd been moved to this tiny box. We replaced each machine with flowers. I recognized roses and daisies and Queen Anne's lace. Other arrangements included orchids and exotic blooms that could have come from another planet.

Late afternoon sunlight slanted through a window that looked over the tops of trees turned red and gold by October frosts. The room itself was nondescript, walls of grayed-green, requisite television bolted at a height guaranteed to be dangerous to people as tall as Bob. But all you noticed was the riot of blooms.

Ten days had passed since an ambulance

screamed its way to the nearest hospital in High Cross with Bonnie. They removed a bullet from below the rib it had broken on impact. She had lost a lot of blood, but Carl was as bad a shot as he was a lousy human being, and the bullet had missed any vital organs. It's possible that my crying out when I saw him shoot her saved Bonnie's life. Instead of making sure she was dead, he'd taken off after me.

"The clincher for the police was when you regained consciousness and told them who had shot you," Bob told her.

"But before that, it was the teeth marks on his hand that kept Louisa out of jail and stopped Carl from disappearing," my cousin added.

"I can't believe he said was you who had shot me," Bonnie told me.

"That surprised me too," I admitted.

"I wish *I'd* had a chance to bite him." She sat propped up in bed against a pile of pillows. Her exquisite bed jacket was knitted of red angora, making her as bright as the most exotic of the flowers.

"He tasted bad, but I admit it was gratifying," I told her. "And there was never any real doubt which one of us started out with the gun. I'm sure Ed knew I didn't have one."

"So tell me again what happened after you got the gun," Bonnie demanded. It was her favorite bedtime story.

"I told him he was toast if he'd killed my dog. I don't even think I'd have needed a gun," I said. "Then Jack barked, and Emily Ann led a parade into the clearing. Kay, and Bob, and Ed, and a highway patrolman I'd never seen before, and Ambrose."

"Emily Ann took us straight through the woods to Louisa. It would have taken hours to find our way without her," Bob said.

"I never realized before that Lassie was really a greyhound in collie makeup, and that Emily Ann is a direct descendent," Kay added.

We all laughed, though this sounded quite plausible to me.

"Go back to the patrolman," Bonnie said. "How did he get into the picture? Bob and Ambrose went to buy coffee and picked up a side of highway patrolman?"

"It was a miracle," Kay stated firmly. "I saw Ambrose's car by the side of the road. A highway patrolman stopped them for speeding."

Ed had told me he was the one who noticed them, since Kay was trying to get a speeding ticket of her own.

"We took too long buying provisions. Ambrose kept meeting people he knew," Bob said. "He spent a lot of time at the cabin with his uncle as a kid."

"It doesn't matter where you go," Kay said, "Ambrose always finds people he knows. Anyway, I did a u-turn and pulled over behind them."

"Then Ed got out and saw that the patrolman was someone he knew," Bob added.

"So I started explaining ("Babbling," Bob said in an aside to me) about bringing Bonnie out to the cabin to see the tape, because I figured if we could get both Ed and George involved, someone would have the jurisdiction and the balls to arrest this son of a bitch."

"Ed finally got everyone into their cars and we all went back to Ambrose's cabin," Bob said.

"And when we got there, Emily Ann came streaking up and Jack took off and we followed Emily Ann to where Louisa had Carl on the ground begging for mercy," Kay finished.

"Not begging for mercy," I corrected. "More like having a wounded panther at my feet ready to tear me apart."

The gun had been steady in my hand as Jack and I stood over Carl. When Jack looked around and barked, I recognized Emily Ann's bark in return. My knees went a little weak at the realization she was alive. I heard large rustling noises and voices coming nearer.

"We're over here," I yelled, careful to keep my attention on Carl.

Emily Ann slid into view, closely followed by Kay and Bob. They ran to me. Kay threw her arms around me while Bob took the gun from my hand and turned to point it at Carl. He wore an expression I had never seen before. Carl quailed at his feet.

"Oh my god, he could have killed you," Kay sobbed. She nearly strangled me with the strength of her hug. I embraced her with relief before I fell to my knees to hug Emily Ann.

"You did it, Emily Ann," I whispered so only she could hear me. "You won the race. You are a good, good girl."

Kay was babbling at me. "Oh, Louisa. How the hell did he get here?"

"He must have followed you," I said.

'I swear I kept an eye out the whole time," she sniffled. "I don't know how he did it."

"It's okay," I said, climbing back to my feet. "He's way sneakier than we are."

Both dogs pricked up their ears. More crashing from the underbrush. Ed stumbled out of the thicket of brush, followed by a uniformed highway patrolman. Finally Ambrose slid into the clearing.

"I love a parade," I said, wondering who else would arrive.

Carl didn't waste a second when he saw the uniformed patrolman. He started to rise. "Officer, thank god you're here. This woman shot my sister-in-law and then attacked me."

"What!" I glared at him.

"I thought she was going to kill me. She must be insane." The indignation in his voice was perfect.

Jack took a couple of stiff-legged steps in his direction and growled at him. He froze in position on his knees. I stare in amazement, but Bob and Kay both turned on him. Bob leaned closer, his knuckles whitening on the gun. Jack began to bark and Kay snarled, "Louisa never! You leave her alone!" Her arms wrapped around me protectively.

The officer, whose name badge read 'G. Smith', raised his hands and commanded, "Stop!"

We all froze.

"He's lying," I said. "He shot Bonnie and he

253

came after me, and Jack jumped him and I got the gun away."

"Not true, officer, she threatened me with the gun. She was pointing it at me when these people—" Carl waved a hand at Kay and Bob—"showed up." He rose to his feet and brushed leaves from the still immaculate creases in his slacks. What did he do, I wondered—run a line of glue down the inside?

Ambrose and Ed had been standing quietly to the side. Ed looked like he was watching amoebas splitting in a petri dish. Ambrose spoke in his most disdainful drawl. "*Louisa* shot someone? I think not, dear boy."

Carl didn't seem to appreciate being a dear boy. "Who are these people?" he burst out, his waspish tone offended.

Ambrose looked down his nose at Carl, but it was the patrolman who spoke. "I am Officer George Smith. And you are?"

Carl brushed a couple of leaves off his sleeve before answering. "Carl Walsh. I happen to be the president of the Trader's Bank and Trust in High Cross, and I also happen to be a close friend of the High Cross chief of police, Tony Saretta."

"Mm-hmm," the patrolman intoned, looking him up and down.

"I demand you arrest this insane woman immediately."

Officer Smith looked Carl up and down. "What's that mark on your wrist?"

Carl was silent.

"I had to bite him to get the gun away from him," I said. Ambrose's eyebrows shot up, and Officer Smith's impassive face gave a brief twitch.

The look on my cousin's face was pure admiration. "You bit him? Way to go, Louisa," she said.

Ed said, "I hope he doesn't have any serious diseases. You didn't get any of his blood on you, did you, Louisa?"

Carl turned red and started to sputter.

"Uh *huh*." Officer Smith studied my face. "Okay. We'll find out more about that later. First, what's this about someone being shot?"

Carl opened his mouth but I spoke first.

"It's Bonnie. He shot her down by the lake. He said he was going to dump both our bodies."

"Did you check her vitals?"

"I—I was up above on a bluff and saw them. I tried to get away but I ended up here, and he was pointing the gun at me."

Carl shook his head, looking disgusted. He opened his mouth to speak again but this time was interrupted by the officer.

"First things first. Let's go," Officer Smith commanded. He made a sweeping motion with his right hand. "Take me to the body."

"*I* don't know how to get there," I told him.

"My cousin never knows where she is," Kay added helpfully.

I frowned at her. "Thanks a lot." I looked around. "I think it's over that way." I pointed.

Officer Smith pursed his lips. "Not if she was

255

shot by the lake. It's in the opposite direction."

"You're quite right, officer." Carl radiated pious distaste. "My poor sister-in-law is down here." He started off, Jack at his heels growling softly. Ed followed them, then Kay, and I tailgated her, Emily Ann at my side. Officer Smith was behind me, and Bob and Ambrose brought up the rear. I looked around at our motley group stringing through the woods and thought that all we needed was a couple of snare drums and a tuba. Carl, with his indignant strut, made a dandy drum major.

The adrenalin that had carried me through my encounter with Carl dissipated. Fatigue crashed down on me. I glanced over my shoulder. Officer Smith kept his hand on the gun in the holster strapped to his side. Of course as soon as I took my eyes off the ground in front of me I stumbled over a rock and nearly fell, but the patrolman leapt forward to grab my arm and keep me on my feet. Bob came to walk behind me, his hand at my waist as he steered me around obstacles.

Carl had to struggle to push through the trees and vines and myanumma bushes. Once he let go of a branch just a little too soon and it whipped back into Kay's face.

"Hey," she growled at him, "do that again and you'll be sorry." Her expression must have convinced him of her sincerity, or perhaps it was Jack's curled lip and barely audible snarl. He took more care after that.

Officer Smith muttered into the radio on his shoulder, I assumed calling for backup. I thought I heard something about hurrying. Suddenly he raised his voice.

"Hey, you're headed away from the lake," he said sternly.

Carl managed to look startled. "Sorry. I'm not used to tramping around in the woods," he said. "Back this way?" He shoved his way through the underbrush, leading us downhill. "I think it's clearing ahead."

The ground leveled out, the trees thinned, and I could see water lapping at the shore. We followed Carl around a curve, and there was Bonnie's body.

I had seen her fall on her back when Carl shot her, but now she lay face down, an ominous pool of blood soaking into the earth under her. The cheerful red plaid of her shirt was stained brown with gore. A trail of blood led to the spot where she had confronted Carl.

Kay pushed Carl aside, sprinted to Bonnie, and flung herself down to feel for a pulse. "She's alive!" she crowed, her face split in a wide smile as she looked back at us.

"And I am," Bonnie said in wonder from her hospital bed. Her smile was as wide as Kay's had been. "Thanks to you all, I'm alive. Bob, kidnapping you may have been the luckiest thing I've ever done."

The smile lines around his eyes crinkled. "Well, shucks, ma'am, it weren't nothin'," he drawled and tipped an imaginary hat. "Pretty darned lucky for me too." We were all silent, thinking about what might have happened. If Bonnie had not snatched Bob, if Carl had found him home alone, Bob would have been armed with nothing more than a low-slung dog. Though having seen Jack in action, I thought that could have been enough.

The door to Bonnie's room opened and Ambrose backed in. He turned, and I saw that he was carrying a tray. "Hello, everyone," he greeted us. "I was here yesterday when they brought Bonnie a meal, and I thought I would spare her another round of gruel and jello." He raised the tray slightly.

We shifted to make a path for him through the room. He set the tray on the rolling cart by Bonnie's bed and swung it over her lap. The tray was exquisite, wooden with an inlaid geometric design of silver. On it rested a china plate decorated in an old-fashioned design of blue and yellow flowers, a yellow linen napkin, heavy shining silverware, and a little nosegay of scented purple violets. The plate held a variety of steamed baby vegetables, a pale green dipping sauce flecked with herbs in a little crystal bowl, and a fragrant fresh bread roll, the brown top shiny with butter. My stomach growled at the sight.

Bonnie lifted the violets to her nose, breathed in and smiled. "This looks wonderful," she said to Ambrose. She reached out and pressed his hand. "Thank you so much. I think one more hospital dinner might have finished off what Carl started." She spread the napkin on her lap and picked up her fork. "I hope you'll excuse me, but this is too tempting. And it feels so marvelous to be alive and *hungry*."

"We've been telling Bonnie what happened after she was shot," Kay told Ambrose.

"We should let her dine in peace," Bob added. "She's much better, but we mustn't tire her."

She hastily swallowed the bite she'd just taken. "Oh, but tell me what's happening now," she said. "Is he still in jail?" When she spoke of Carl, she didn't need to use his name. Her voice took on an edge that could cut glass.

I nodded. "They made a case that he's a flight risk."

Kay said, "His lawyer tried to argue that Carl's a pillar of the community, but the judge looked at how much money he has and decided to keep him in jail."

"Quite right," Bonnie sniffed. "Of course he would run away. He would set up a new identity somewhere else and ruin other lives."

"That's assuming he could have sneaked past the news media," Bob said. He looked at me and shook his head. "No wonder you were leery of me when you thought I might be a reporter."

I smiled at him. "You considered my reaction exaggerated, admit it."

"I don't know if Bob did, but I thought you were nuts," my loving cousin said frankly. "I mean, I knew you'd been hurt by Roger and that you're, well, sensitive—"

"Thin skinned, touchy, you can say it," I told her.

Kay nodded. "Okay, thin skinned and touchy. But geez, this has been a zoo." She turned to Bonnie. "They put guards on your door right away to keep the media out. Did you know that by the time the ambul-

259

ance got you to the hospital, reporters were already here?"

"I'm afraid I wasn't paying much attention at the time," Bonnie said. "Is that why everyone stayed away for days? The news media?"

"That, plus you weren't ready to entertain," Ambrose said. "But eat your nice veggies and you'll be better in no time."

"The media scrum wasn't just here," I said. "Ambrose rode with you in the ambulance, and another patrol car came for Carl, and the rest of us went to the Willow Falls Police Station in Officer Smith's car. Half a dozen news vans arrived before us."

"They love things like a bank president running amok, shooting people in the woods and being bitten by one of his intended victims," Kay said.

Bob added, "Just when we thought things were cooling off, word got out that some of the High Cross police might be involved. And they were off again."

Kay began to laugh. "You should have seen Louisa on the news that first night. They caught her getting out of the patrol car. She had blood smeared on her face, and mud, and leaves in her hair."

"While Carl was all neat and clean on the film, and he still had those obnoxious creases in his pants," I said bitterly. "I looked far more evil than he did."

Bob looked at me. "Creases?"

"At least Emily Ann looked beautiful," I added, giving Bob an 'I'll tell you later' look.

"And now," Kay said, "they are talking about a movie of the week loosely based on what happened."

"Loosely?" Bonnie asked.

"Apparently the real thing wasn't cinematic enough," I explained. "Probably no good camera angles among the myanumma bushes."

"But the good news is that the store got so much press," Kay went on, "that we've sold so much I may have to close for a couple of weeks to find more inventory. And Ambrose and Bob have more business than they can handle. Even that oak monstrosity in the restaurant in High Cross is famous."

A tap on the door. Officer George Smith stuck his head in, noted the group in the room, and entered. He held the door for Ed to follow. The room was as full as the proverbial sardine can. Bob and I retreated to the window and leaned hip-to-hip on the sill. Ed threaded his way to Bonnie and shook her hand. "You're looking much better," he told her with a crinkly smile, and I saw Bonnie squeeze his hand and smile in return. I began to understand what Kay saw in him. That smile was disarming.

Officer Smith shook hands with Ambrose and Kay, and smiled across the room and nodded to Bob and me. "Good, you're all here," he said. "Ed and I were going to start with Mrs. Becker, and I planned to call the rest of you in the morning."

"What's up?" Bob asked.

The officer looked at Bonnie. "We just heard from the detectives working on your case."

All eyes were riveted on him.

"They've broken Walsh's alibi for the night his stepson died."

Bonnie's quick intake of breath was loud in the silence that followed. Ed took up the narrative. "He claimed to have spent the night in a hotel in Kansas City. He had dinner with a young woman, and took her back to his room. We think he drugged her dinner. She passed out shortly after they went upstairs."

Officer Smith nodded. "We've ascertained that Carl rented a motorcycle under an assumed name earlier in the day, and that's how he got back to High Cross in the night."

"A motorcycle!" Bonnie exclaimed.

"With the helmet on, no one he passed on the road would recognize him."

"Then how—?" I began.

"The guy at the motorcycle shop picked his picture out of half a dozen that we showed him, and the woman he took to his room will testify that she doesn't remember if he was there all night." Officer Smith gave a satisfied smile.

"*And* a police report was filed that night," Ed added. "One of the neighbors complained about a dog making a lot of noise at Walsh's house." He looked at Bob. "Your dog must have done his best to get to Walsh, but he was locked out of the house."

I swallowed hard at the thought of Jack futilely trying to get into the house to protect Ian that night. It was too vivid, and I pushed the image away. If only he could have saved Ian's life, as he undoubtedly had saved mine.

Officer Smith's voice was sober as he went on, "The DA thinks she has a real good chance of convicting him of Ian's death at least, as well as your attempted murder, Mrs. Becker. They are still working on the night your sister died, but we'll be able to put him away even without that."

Bonnie carefully laid her fork down beside her plate and sat very still, her face tilted away from my view. She looked back, tears sliding down her cheeks. "Oh. God. Oh, thank you, George. And you, Ed. Nothing can bring back my sister or my nephew. But the pain of knowing he'd killed them and gotten away with it was even worse."

I felt my own tears about to spill over. I blinked hard. Kay reached for the box of tissues on the bedside table and handed a couple to Bonnie. Ed took the box from her and gave it to me. He gave me a little pat on the shoulder, which threatened my composure even more. I blew my nose harder than I intended, and the honking noise raised a relieved laugh from everyone. "Oops, sorry," I said. "That's great news." I handed the tissue box back to Ed.

"Get ready for more reporters," he said, and Officer Smith nodded. "I understand the DA is planning a press conference for tomorrow morning."

"Here we go again," remarked Kay. "I can hardly wait to see the movie they make out of this thing."

"I doubt if we'll recognize it," I said.

Kay nodded. "Carl's rented Kawasaki will become a roaring Harley, and the actor playing him will have to have long hair so it can stream out dramatically in the moonlight."

Ed grinned at the image. He turned to Bonnie,

who suddenly looked exhausted. "Hey, you need to rest," he said. "You're still pretty pale."

"I'm all right," she said staunchly.

"You need to rest," he said again.

Officer Smith said, "They'll be here from the DA's office here tomorrow to talk to you." Bonnie nodded, and sighed.

Ed turned to my cousin. "You ready to go, Kay?"

"Go?" I inquired, giving Kay a look over the tops of my glasses. Her expression was particularly bland.

"Ed invited me to dinner," she said, picking up her purse.

"How nice." I kept my tone dry to keep from laughing.

"Yes. We have some things to talk about." She went to Bonnie and gave her a kiss on the cheek. "I'll be back tomorrow," she promised, and she and Ed were out the door.

"We need to be going, too," George said. He was looking at Ambrose. "I was able to get those theatre tickets we talked about, and we have a reservation for dinner. Mrs. Becker, good luck with the DA tomorrow. I hope I'll see you soon."

Ambrose smiled and waved to us as he went through the door, closely followed by George. Bonnie and Bob and I looked at each other.

"Well," I said. And couldn't think of anything to add.

Bonnie nodded. "This is turning out to be the proverbial ill wind," she said, "blowing more good than

I would ever have thought possible."

I looked from Bob to Bonnie and promised, "I'll pry all the interesting details out of Kay and Ambrose tomorrow."

"We need to be going too," Bob told Bonnie. "We have to feed the dogs, not to mention ourselves." He turned toward the door, then stopped. "Oh, I just remembered. One loose end hasn't been tied up."

Bonnie and I both looked at him.

"We still don't know who Trixie is," he explained.

"That's right," I said.

"Frankly, it's driving me crazy. Do you mind if I use the phone? Her number will probably be busy, but I might as well try it one more time."

"Be my guest," said Bonnie, who had heard about the matchbook and the elusive Trixie. "I'm as curious as anyone."

Bob sat down in the room's single chair and pulled the phone on the bedside table closer to him. He dialed Trixie's number quickly; we had all memorized it in the past few days from trying it repeatedly. As Bob had said, so far it had always been busy. I was convinced it was lying off the hook on a floor somewhere in an abandoned building. This time, however, a big smile soon creased his face.

"It's ringing!" he hissed at Bonnie and me. He sat up straighter and tightened his grip on the receiver. "Hello? Yes, this is Bob Richardson. May I speak to Trixie, please? Oh, good, I'm so glad to have gotten hold of you. Your line seems to be busy all the

265

time...Say, do you mind if I put you on the speaker-phone? I wear a hearing aid and it's easier to use the phone that way...Thanks."

Bonnie and I looked at each other. Hearing aid? "Great excuse to let us listen," she whispered.

Apparently Trixie agreed, and Bob touched the button to turn on the speaker. "Can you hear me okay now?"

"I sure can." The woman's voice held a country sound. I could imagine her sitting at a farmhouse kitchen table covered by a red checked cloth. "I'm sorry, could you tell me who you are again?"

I perched beside Bonnie on the edge of her bed. We made shushing gestures at each other.

"My name is Bob Richardson. You don't know me, but several days ago, someone left a matchbook at my house with your name and phone number written inside the cover..."

I could hear the instant defensiveness in her tone. "Well, and just what did you think you'd find when you called the number? Just 'cause a woman gives her number to someone doesn't mean—"

"Oh, no, please," Bob jumped in. "I really didn't make any assumptions. I'm trying to figure out who the heck had been in my house and left these matches. They're from a bar I've never been to."

"A bar, huh," she said.

"I have a friend who needs to know I haven't been going to places she might not like."

She gave a laugh that came from the belly. "Oh, I got it. Your lady friend saw a book of matches from a

bar with my name written inside and started gettin'
her exercise by jumpin' to conclusions."

Bob chuckled. "Something like that. So anyway,
the matches are from a bar called The Last Resort—"

"Was the writing in purple ink?"

"Yes! Yes it was! Do you remember who you
might have given it to? I'm hoping we can follow the
trail and find out who left them at my house."

"Well, the trail might be kinda short, because I
do know whose matches I wrote on. Fella named Clay
Harburn. His family owns that bar, and his grandma
runs it. But she's getting the Alzheimer's so bad that
the grandsons take turns bein' at the bar when she's
there. Most of the time anymore she just thinks
they're another customer. It's awful sad, really. Clay
takes the afternoon shift since he's not workin'. I don't
think anyone's ever gonna give him a job if he won't
learn to cover up that big ol' tattoo on his arm. Anyway, I gave him my number to give to his brother, because he had something to sell that I was thinking
about buying. And his brother works for the gas company. I don't suppose you had anyone from the gas
company out to your place around that time?"

Bob started laughing. "Yes! Yes! I had the fur-
nace checked for the winter and the pilot light relit."

"Well, that's it then. Clay's brother Harden
must have been the one who was there and he used
those matches to light the pilot and laid 'em down and
forgot 'em."

"That must be exactly what happened. So simple when you have an explanation. This is certainly a

relief."

"Unless Harden gave 'em to a burglar, but I don't think he hardly had time."

"Probably not," Bob agreed. "I was imagining all kinds of weird ways those matches could have gotten there. And Louisa has an even better imagination." He gave me a private smile across the room. Bonnie poked me in the ribs. "I really thank you for talking to me. I know it must have seemed strange for me to call you."

"Oh, that's okay," she said, "as long as you didn't think I was some kind of loose woman or something. It's kind of nice to actually talk to someone."

"Really? Your phone line is busy so much of the time, you must have plenty of people to talk to."

She laughed again. "You prob'ly think I'm the biggest ol' gossip in the state, but it's my computer that's been doin' all the talkin', not me. I buy and sell stuff on the Internet, so I'm online most of the time. I gotta get me a better connection one of these days."

"I see," Bob said.

"In fact, that's why I gave my number to Clay to give to Harden. He inherited a collection of Barbie dolls from their aunt and I was goin' to sell it for him. At least that's what they say. They may be big ol' country boys but I kinda think them Barbies might have been Harden's all along."

"Their secret is safe with me," Bob promised. "Thank you so much for talking with me, Trixie. I hope our paths cross again sometime."

"Maybe they will, you just never know. You

take care now."

"You too," Bob said, and started to disconnect.

"Oh, and Mr. Richardson..."

"Yes?"

"That hearing aid of yours didn't show up at all when they interviewed you on the news." We heard her laughing as she hung up.

Bob pushed the button on the phone and looked at us. "I'd say game, set and matches to Trixie, wouldn't you?"

32

The next day was a beautiful autumn Saturday: clear and crisp, festooned with colorful falling leaves. Bob and I held hands as we walked along Maple Street. Emily Ann paced demurely at my side, and Jack investigated the smells on the sidewalk.

"So Monday's the big day?"

Bob nodded. "I've got a full schedule of appointments for the next month. All my Monday, Tuesday, and Wednesday times are full. I've decided I won't take any for the end of the week. I'll mostly commute from here for now, though I'll need to spend a night at my place in High Cross once in a while."

"I hope they're people who really need help and not weirdoes who saw you on the news."

He shrugged. "Oh, some of them may be, but maybe those are the ones who need the most help. Once they see me in person they'll realize how ordinary I am."

We passed the store with the old radios, and the toy store. "I don't know, I think you're pretty extraordinary." We exchanged a private smile. "And I've kind of gotten used to having you around. But at least Jack will get to spend the days with us." Hearing his name, Jack looked up at me and wagged. "You'll make a wonderful antique salesman," I told him. "You can demonstrate couches like Emily Ann does. Or perhaps you could specialize in our overstuffed chairs."

Bob squeezed my hand. "Oh, I'll still be around," he assured me, and the look he gave me sent an involuntary shiver down my back all the way to my toes.

We were on our way to the Bluebird for a late morning cinnamon roll. We had slept in, but the thought of sweet, spicy bread had pulled us out of my house and down to Maple.

As we neared the yarn shop across the street from Kay's place I noticed a new display in the window, and we stopped to take a look. Three teddy bears wearing hand-knit sweaters in bright fall colors were having a picnic. Miniature dishes were spread on a beautiful woolen afghan, and the floor around it was piled with real autumn leaves in reds and yellows. The baby teddy reached for a leaf that was suspended in mid-air, and I gave a little chuckle when I saw it, for it wore bright emerald green angora mittens on its ears.

"Oh, look at the mittens," I said to Bob. Then the morning air was split by my shouted name.

"Louisa! Oh, LEW-EEEE-SA! Is that you?" It was Doris, hailing me once more from across Maple

Street.

"Oh. My. God," I growled. I turned to see her hurrying toward us. "I don't believe this. Does she *never* go home?" Bob's grip on my hand tightened reassuringly.

"Well!" she said brightly when she reached us. "We meet again."

"Yes," I said. "What are you doing here?"

"I'm working for a client with interests in St. Joseph."

"Ah."

"It was a good opportunity to come back down here. I see you're still with Mr. Dickson—"

"Richardson," I corrected.

"Oh yes, Richardson." Her tone grew arch. "It's unbelievable, what you've been up to! Some people will do anything for attention." Her smile would have frightened any jury, and could probably cause someone in the witness box to faint.

I felt Bob draw in breath to speak, but I squeezed his hand and he waited.

"I was with Humphrey, you remember, Louisa, Roger's senior partner, when we saw you on the news. You looked like you'd just rolled down a muddy hillside."

"I had," I said.

"I told Humphrey thank heavens Roger isn't here. He would die all over again to see his wife looking like that on national television. Really, Louisa, if I were you I would sue them for—"

"Doris," I said. She swept on.

272

"—sue them for broadcasting film of you looking like that! Everyone agreed that—"

I tried again. "Doris!"

"—well, it was natural for you to have let yourself go after you lost Roger. I mean, his death was traumatic in *so* many ways, no doubt it just sent you off the deep end, but—"

"DORIS!" Shouting finally had the desired effect; she was silenced. Heads snapped around to stare at us all along Maple Street, and Jack rose to put his front paws on my leg. "It's okay, Jack," I assured him, and gave Bob a smile before looking at Doris again.

"Good morning, Doris. Yes, it is a beautiful day, and how nice that you were able to come back to Willow Falls and do some more shopping. I know that all the merchants on Maple Street are thrilled to have your business, except, of course, for the proprietress of OKay Antiques. I happen to know that she would not let you through the door." I gave her a warm smile.

"Well!" she bridled, but I held up a hand to stop her.

"Yes, it is hard to believe what happened," I swept on, "and Roger would certainly have hated seeing me on the news. But I hated seeing him in real life and anyway he's dead, so my notoriety is no problem. And you have to admit mine pales in comparison to his."

"Louisa!" she gasped.

Interrupting her gave me a heady sense of joy. I could feel Bob shaking with silent laughter. "Doris, the past couple of weeks have taught me a lot about myself, things I might never have known otherwise." I took a moment to look her up and down. "One thing really stands out in my mind, though. Something I wish I'd known years ago."

I gathered up Emily Ann's leash in preparation for continuing down the street. She stood, noble, graceful, with Jack at her side, short and silly and perpetually wagging his tail. Doris glanced at them before meeting my eyes.

"Yes? What is it that you've learned?" Her voice was less strident than I'd ever heard it before.

I smiled at her, lifted my chin, and took the first step down Maple Street.

"I bite."

THE END

About the author:

Sharon Henegar wrote and illustrated her first book at the age of nine. It was about wild horses. She has had a long career as a children's librarian, and is looking forward to just as many years as a novelist. She has completed three books in the Willow Falls series, and is currently uncovering a plot involving a cat named Fig. She lives in California and Oregon with her storyteller husband, dogs Lizzie and Edward, and cats Noll Baxter and Mrs. Wilberforce.

On Saturday mornings she pursues her avocation of thrifting in her green convertible. Follow her adventures as the Queen of Fifty Cents on her website (http://queenoffiftycents.blogspot.com/).

Need more copies of
Sleeping Dogs Lie?

Order today from
Saturday Books
www.SaturdayBooks.com

And watch for the next
Willow Falls Mystery,
coming soon:

In Dogs We Trust